HOME AGAIN

THE LONG ROAD HOME

CAITLYN O'LEARY

Cover by Cat Johnson Design
Edited by Rebecca Hodgkins
Content Edited by Trenda Lundin
Cover Photo by: Wander Aguiar :: Photography

❀ Created with Vellum

To those who are serving and those who have served.

SYNOPSIS

Can he solve the mystery that has haunted him for years and set things right before it crumbles down around him and the woman who's become entangled in his mess?

Since two days before Sebastian's eighteenth birthday, when he left home to join the Navy, he's been running away from the pain, the confusion, the terror, and the guilt.

But the Navy had made a man out of him, and now it was time to finally come to terms with his past, so he was going back.

When he finds a new woman in town, unknowingly caught up in the chaos of his past, Sebastian knows time is running out. Then he finds himself entangled with Gianna on a much more personal basis and he wants time to stand still.

Can he unravel the past and grab onto the future before it's too late?

1

Sebastian Durand stood well away from the luggage carousel even though he could see his duffel bag over the heads of the men, women, and children in front of him. There wasn't a chance in hell he was going to push his way to the front; standing back and watching was far more interesting.

"Stay away. Let me do it." A pouty little blonde-haired toddler said emphatically to her harassed father as she made her third attempt to grab her tiny Hello Kitty suitcase off the carousel.

"Lexi, leave it, I'll get it when it comes around next time," the man in chinos and a polo shirt said distractedly. He turned to a boy who must have been his son who was holding an iPad and wandering toward a vending machine. "Robert, come back here," he called out loudly.

When the man's back was turned, the little girl pulled herself up on the ledge of the carousel and swung one chubby leg over the stainless steel rim. She was clearly planning on chasing after her suitcase.

Sebastian pushed his way forward. He grabbed the little girl up by her waist and snagged the Hello Kitty bag.

"I wanna do it!" the girl shrieked.

The man turned around and saw Sebastian setting his daughter down on the floor.

"Give me Kitty," she demanded as she thrust her hands on her hips. Sebastian had to stop himself from laughing.

"What's going on?" the man asked over his shoulder as he made a lunge for his son who was three meters in front of him.

"That guy saved your daughter from a fall, is what's going on," a woman with a bad dye job said.

The father dragged his son back to his daughter and glared at Sebastian. "You put your hands on my daughter?" he yelled.

Sebastian took a deep breath.

No good deed goes unpunished. Here it comes.

Sebastian knew the type well; how many newly minted lieutenants had he had to listen to over the years, who thought they knew something when they clearly had shit for brains?

Too many.

He kept his expression blank as the man, about his height, stared daggers at him, holding each of his kids by their wrists as they struggled in his grip.

"Asshole, you had no right to touch my girl."

"Dad, let go, you're hurting me," the boy said as he used his free hand to try to peel off his dad's fingers. At this rate, the father was going to leave bruises on his kids' wrists.

"Somebody had to act like a parent," some soccer-type mom piped up as she came to stand next to Sebastian. "And don't hold onto your kids so tight."

"I'll do whatever the hell I want to do, lady."

The little girl dropped her suitcase handle and looked

up at her father. She started to whimper. "Why are you mad, Daddy?"

"Don't ever touch somebody's kids," the man growled at Sebastian. "I bet you think you're some kind of tough guy, right?"

"Mister, you need to get your luggage and stop manhandling your kids." The spirited soccer mom tried to get between Sebastian and the pissed-off dad.

"Look, bitch..."

"Enough." Sebastian's voice was low and menacing as he gently moved the mom out of the way. He took a step forward and leaned into the father. "Get yourself under control," he whispered. "Your kids are watching, don't give them a bad memory."

The man twisted his head backwards and Sebastian leaned into him a little more.

"Let go of your kids' wrists, kneel down, hug 'em, say you're sorry, get your luggage, and every day of your life thank your fuckin' stars you've been blessed by God for them. You get me?"

Sebastian watched as all color leached out of the man's face, then he gave Sebastian a nod. Sebastian stepped out of the asshole's space and watched with narrowed eyes as the guy knelt down and did exactly what he'd told him to do. When he witnessed the hug and saw that it seemed genuine, he turned back to the carousel and snagged his duffel.

He glanced once more at the guy and his children and saw that both of the kids were smiling. He breathed a little easier.

As he headed toward the exit on the main concourse he heard a woman yell, "Wait up."

Sebastian turned and saw the petite soccer mom

smiling at him, so he stopped and arched his eyebrow in question.

"Thank you," she said quietly.

"Hmmm?"

"You did right back there." She reached up and squeezed his bicep. "Not enough right in the world, but you did it, so thank you." She smiled, then turned and left.

For the first time in what felt like forever, Sebastian felt like he might get through the next few weeks.

Sebastian arched his neck, trying to loosen his muscles. This was the third uncomfortable chair near the third gate he'd been assigned to in the last five hours, and he didn't know why he was bothering. He looked up at the floor-to-ceiling window in front of him and watched the rain slash sideways. Why they even tried to say the planes were just delayed was a mystery to him. Hurricane Helen was going to cancel everything here at the Atlanta airport, so they might as well just call it.

His phone vibrated, so he pulled it out of his back pocket, hoping it might be one of his teammates. It wasn't. It was his grandfather, one of the last people on earth he wanted to talk to, so he let the call go to voicemail. It was bad enough he had to see the bastard in the very near future; there wasn't a chance in hell he was going to talk to him anytime beforehand. Just having the old man's damn letter in his pocket was giving him hives.

"Canceled?" the woman to the right of him screeched. He looked at her out of the corner of his eye.

Really? She was surprised?

Sebastian picked up his duffel and headed left. He'd already scoped out where the USO was. He probably should have headed there hours ago, but there'd been something soothing about the storm that called to him. The outer turmoil matched what he was feeling inside.

He followed the stream of people toward the Airport Atrium. They were slow, but there was no rush. He'd probably end up sleeping on the floor at the USO, which was a hell of a lot better than where he'd slept on his last mission.

By the time he got to the third floor, he was once again thinking about the old house in Lafourche Parish. When he got to the desk a tall, older woman with a Texas accent was talking to a woman in a combat uniform standing beside a tall man in jeans and a Broncos shirt. The man was holding the woman's duffel and had his arm around her waist. Both of them wore wedding bands.

"Let me see if I can get you situated with some food."

"No need, Blessing, this isn't our first rodeo," the woman said. "Pete picked me up some barbeque before dropping off the rental car."

The man held up a white bag with grease stains and the older woman grinned. "Well, y'all know the way back. Remember, don't get *too* comfortable," she teased the young couple.

The Broncos fan let out a big laugh as his wife buried her face into his chest. They wandered down the hall and Blessing turned to Sebastian with a twinkle in her eye. Despite the angst he'd been feeling about going home, he couldn't help but return her smile.

"Hello, Blessing," he held out his hand. "I'm Sebastian Durand."

She took his hand in hers. "Welcome to the Atlanta USO. Do I hear a little of the bayou in your voice?" she asked before walking behind the desk to check him in.

Sebastian nodded. "Lafourche Parish, Louisiana. I'm on leave, heading back for a while."

Blessing gave a slight frown. "So that's home?"

"It was where I was raised," Sebastian qualified.

"Family there?"

He rubbed the back of his neck. "Some."

She came around from the back of the desk, put her hand on his bicep, and looked up at him. "How long has it been since you've been back to Louisiana?" she asked quietly.

"Twelve years," he admitted. "Didn't think I'd ever go back." Sebastian stopped short, amazed he'd admitted something like that to a stranger.

Her eyes searched his. "You'll be able to handle this, Sebastian. I know it."

Sebastian's head shot up in shock. "I beg your pardon?"

"God doesn't give us more than we can handle. What's more, it's finally your time to go back. You're going to find that not only will you get the answers you've always needed, you're going to find joy."

Sebastian's eyebrows shot up. "Uhmm."

Blessing's laugh sounded like bells. "It's okay, never mind me. I'll just take you back and find you someplace comfortable to weather out the storm. Follow me." She took two steps expecting him to follow her.

"Wait, how do you know I need answers?"

Shit, what was wrong with him? Why should he care what this woman said? But, how in the hell could she have possibly known that he was going for that very reason?

She turned back to him, her expression holding such warmth and caring. "Sebastian, I'm not sure how I know, but I know." Once again she reached out and squeezed his arm. "Trust. I know it's not in your nature, but try to open yourself up to trust, okay?" She kept staring at him until he finally nodded.

"This way," she said as she turned toward the hallway.

He followed her down a red, white, and blue striped hall, lost in thought until she pointed to a shelving unit. "You can set your duffel there." Sebastian nodded and shelved his bag, then continued to follow her as they ended up in an almost empty room that had some brown leather furniture. The only one there was a scowling man with his foot in a black walking boot.

"I'd like to introduce you two. Sebastian Durand, this is Kyle Jones who is also in the Navy."

Kyle started to push up from the couch and Sebastian shook his head. Kyle settled back down with a brief nod. "Blessing, how'd you know I was in the Navy?" Sebastian asked.

Shit, does she know his middle name too?

"I saw your name and rank on your duffel luggage tag," she smiled. "Anyway, I'll leave you two gentleman alone to get better acquainted. Bye, y'all." Sebastian stared after her as he sank down on the couch across from Kyle.

"Where you stationed?" Sebastian asked Kyle after a few minutes of silence.

"Coronado," Kyle answered.

Sebastian wasn't surprised. Kyle had the special ops feel to him.

"You?" Kyle asked.

"Little Creek," Sebastian said. He waited to see if Kyle was going to ask questions since it was obvious they were both Navy SEALs, but he didn't. Maybe Kyle was going home to a big ole' pile of shit too. Sebastian's lip curled up.

"What you smiling about?" Kyle asked.

Sebastian considered giving him a one-word answer, but a little conversation *would* make time go faster. "Thinking about the bullshit I'm going back to. Thinking our shitty moods match."

Kyle's lips twitched. "Dude, you're reading me wrong if

you think this is a shitty mood. This is me on a good day, especially since this shit happened." Kyle lifted his injured leg and grimaced.

Sebastian laughed, then winced as he once again looked at Kyle's broken ankle. He could really get to like this guy. They continued to talk. Nothing too deep; Sebastian wasn't in the mood to unload on Kyle. It was bad enough having to go home, and he could tell that Kyle had his own reasons for keeping things to himself…still. They ended up sharing contact information before Blessing brought in more men. Before the night was over there were five of them. Five good men who ended up making Sebastian feel he was in a much better space before having to return to a place he'd vowed never to see again in his life.

2

Now, this *is Louisiana hurricane weather,* Sebastian thought with a grimace. He'd hoped that after spending the night stuck in the Atlanta airport that Hurricane Helen would have wound down a little bit more, but she was proving to be a bitch. The rain wasn't hitting the rental SUV on the roof, it was hitting the passenger door and the wind was doing its damndest to push him off the freeway. He was debating whether or not to pull over when he saw the turnoff for Highway One. He went over a lane so he could take the exit. All in all, it wasn't any worse than any of the sandstorms he'd experienced overseas. In fact, those sandstorms had kind of reminded him of hurricanes.

He tried the radio one last time with no results, then pushed the car into the lowest gear possible and continued on down the highway towards the place he'd been forced to live after his mother died. Under normal circumstances, it would have taken him a half-hour to hit Larose after hopping off the Ninety, but at this rate, it would take a couple of hours. Probably for the best; this way he'd have even more time to get in the right frame of mind. The old man's letter had hit him like a bolt of lightning last week.

Sebastian gripped the steering wheel even harder. Mostly it had been the same old song and dance, Grand-père busy being the wily old puppet master. But this time the old bastard had thrown in the one thing he knew that Sebastian couldn't resist.

Answers. Answers to questions that had been plaguing him for over twenty years.

He might've been a child at the time, but Sebastian knew what he'd heard. Back then, it hadn't made any sense, but when his mother had been killed weeks later, he'd confronted his dad and his grandfather. They'd told him he'd misunderstood their argument and he should just forget it. But he couldn't. Not then and not now.

After his mother's death, he'd no longer had the respite to spend the weekdays at her house. Instead, he'd then had to spend every single day with his father, uncle, and Grandpère at the Durand family home. He'd hated it; he'd felt sad, empty, and lost. It had gotten a thousand times worse when months later, his dad's car had ended up in the swamp.

It took another half-hour before he got closer to the Valentine Bridge and his hands started to sweat. He didn't need this. Sebastian wiped the perspiration off on his jeans, before clutching his steering wheel again. He'd hated crossing this bridge every fucking time since his father's death, but to do it in a storm was a whole new dimension of hell.

Sebastian squinted as the old lift bridge started to come into focus. Even through the pouring rain, he could make out the towers on the north side of the bridge. It'd been on a night like this that his dad's BMW Z8 had missed the entrance to the bridge and sailed into Bayou Lafourche.

They'd tried to keep Sebastian from reading the newspaper article about Sebastian Durand the Third, but the little shit Andy Beaumont had brought it into school for him to read. The words *sailed over* were burned into Sebastian's brain. So were the pictures of his dad's car being pulled out of the bayou.

Down to a snail's pace, Sebastian started over the tiny bridge, remembering the hundreds of times he'd ridden with his father in his prized sports car as a boy. Now thinking back on those times from a man's point of view, he knew damn good and well that his father was a good driver. Scratch that, an *excellent* driver. There wasn't a chance in fucking hell that he wouldn't have made it onto the bridge no matter how bad of a storm he'd been in.

For the thousandth time, Sebastian wondered if his father had been drinking or had been high that night. There'd been no mention of it in the papers, and of course, nobody was going to tell an eight-year-old kid that his father had been messed up when he'd crashed his car. After both of his parents were dead, his life at the Durand family home became a misery. It was a life that he'd longed to escape.

Sebastian forced himself to concentrate on the here and now, looking at the bridge in his rearview mirror. At most, he would be at the family home in an hour. He started to count in his head, a coping mechanism from his childhood. Something that would soothe him and remind him that time would eventually pass.

Sebastian snorted out a laugh, imagining what his teammates Gideon Smith or Keegan Harris would say to him if they saw his panties in such a twist. He needed to get his shit together. He wasn't a kid anymore, nor was he the eighteen-year-old teenager who'd stormed out of Lafourche twelve years ago.

Just like that, the tension bled out of his body, and he hadn't even needed bourbon. Then, as if the weather caught onto his mood, the rain started to let up. Not a lot, but enough so that he could see a little bit better.

"Shit."

Sebastian grinned when he saw the green neon sign of Jimmy's Po-Boys off to his right. Trust Jimmy to be open in the middle of a hurricane. That meant the power was still on in their little town, unless Jimmy was running his restaurant off of a generator, which was possible. He wondered if a generator had been installed at the Durand residence. After so many hurricanes you'd think that would've been an investment they could've made. Of course, the only money that Sebastian Lazar Durand the Second ever wanted to spend was on something that would win him an election.

Before leaving Virginia, Sebastian had done an internet search to see what the old man was up to. He didn't know why he was surprised to find out he'd moved from his position as a state representative to the president of the state senate and was now campaigning for lieutenant governor. Actually, he was surprised; he would've thought by now that his grandfather would be gunning for the Governor's mansion. Then again, maybe he realized that at seventy-four, he was too old for the job.

Sebastian blasted the car's air conditioner as he drove the last ten miles to hell. He tensed as he took the turn off of the highway onto the farm road. He sighed as he passed the sugarcane fields on his left and wondered if the devastation of Hurricane Helen was going to make any of the farmers go under. Finally, he could see the turn-off to the Durand farm up ahead. He knew the dirt road was going to be a muddy mess; thank God there had been an SUV to rent instead of some damned sedan.

After twenty minutes on the muddy drive, he finally spotted the house that had been built in nineteen-ten. There was only one car parked in front—a current-year Cadillac of course—the old man's tastes hadn't changed in the slightest. Sebastian pulled in near the side of the house. He ran up the stairs to the front door, thankful for the covered porch; at least he had a little bit of coverage while he hit the doorbell and pounded on the thick wood, hoping that his Grandpère would hear one or the other. After three minutes of nobody answering, he tried the doorknob and found the door unlocked. Hell, he should've tried that from the get-go.

Walking into the foyer after so much time was mind-boggling, and as soon as that scent of lemon hit him, Sebastian knew that Ophelia had to still be working for the family. She'd always insisted on using lemon oil when cleaning the maple floors. He wandered into the foyer and peeked into the drawing-room off to the right. It was empty of people, but the grand piano was still there. God only knew why his grandfather kept it, since the only person who had ever played it had been his grandmother, and she'd died forty years ago.

"Hello," he shouted up the grand staircase. Nobody answered, but somebody must belong to the Cadillac. Then there was the fact that the house was lit up like a Christmas tree. His grandfather was too cheap to have all these lights on if the house was empty. Sebastian shouted again and still didn't get an answer. He wasn't going to check out the kitchen because he couldn't imagine that Ophelia would be here cooking or cleaning during a hurricane; she had her own family to take care of. The old man was probably huddled away in his study trying to take over the state of Louisiana. Sebastian sauntered down the hall behind the staircase and knocked on the study door. No answer. He pushed it open.

"Daddy, what are you doing home? Aren't you supposed to be at the capitol?" It had been so long since Sebastian had been home that it took a minute to decipher the drunken, Creole accent. But he finally understood what had been said.

Uncle Armand shoved himself up from the leather couch and tried to stand up straight, but he was missing the mark. He was drunker than a skunk.

"I'm not your daddy," Sebastian responded easily.

Armand squinted then fell back onto the couch, kicking over the half-full glass that had been on the carpet beside the couch. The man didn't even notice the mess he'd made.

"Who are you? What are you doing in my house?"

"Grandpère invited me for a visit. I would have thought a man who gets the senior discount at the movies wouldn't call his father Daddy, or still be living with him for that matter."

Armand squinted again, obviously trying to get Sebastian into focus. "Is that you, Bastian?"

God how he hated that name. Since joining the Navy he'd either been Sebastian or occasionally Seb. Never, ever Bastian. Of course, a couple of his teammates had found out his middle name and made one attempt to call him Lazar, but after a well-placed punch, that had immediately stopped.

"The name is Sebastian, Uncle."

"Does Daddy know you're coming?"

Sebastian rolled his eyes. No point in explaining himself again, it was a lost cause.

"How long is the old man expected to be at the state capitol?" Sebastian asked.

"He's not due back for another two days. He's meeting

with some lobbyists from Washington D.C. They're a big deal. Going to help him with his campaign. But it's hush-hush, just between us family. Can't tell no one, cause there's some local fellas that'd be pretty pissed off if they found out that Daddy was planning on doing an end-run around them."

Armond made a motion to zip his lips and throw away the key.

Jesus, am I back in elementary school?

Goddammit, he'd left a message with the old man that he'd be here today, but did he bother to be around? Fuck no. It was just another mind game, another way to show how important Lazar Durand was.

Sebastian turned around and started out the door.

"Where are you going?" Armand whined.

"The kitchen."

"You're not going to stay here, are you?"

"Yep."

Sebastian wasn't all that surprised that by the time he was opening the refrigerator, Armand was staggering into the kitchen. "What do you mean you're staying? You don't live here."

"No I don't, thank God." Sebastian pulled out some fried chicken that Ophelia must have left, as well as some potato salad. Now, *this* was living. When he went to grab a beer he grimaced when he saw his only choice was Old Dixie Beer. That had always been the beer of choice in the Durand household. It was brewed in New Orleans, and Lazar loved anything that allowed him to cling to the old South. In his years away from home, Sebastian's tastes had changed, preferring IPAs to lagers, so he grabbed Ophelia's pitcher of lemonade.

"What, our beer isn't good enough for you?" Armand slurred. "Daddy bought up all the old cases of Dixie Beer they had before they changed the name to some Yankee name."

"Now why doesn't that surprise me?" Sebastian muttered. He went about fixing himself a plate of food. He wished Ophelia were here; thinking about her was the only thing about coming home worthwhile. He plunked his plate down on the kitchen table and used his foot to pull out a chair and sat down.

"We eat in the dining room," Armand tried to tutor him.

Once again Sebastian ignored the man, concentrating instead on herbs and spices that exploded in his mouth as he chewed the chicken.

"Are you listening to me?"

Sebastian's head shot up as wind and rain burst into the kitchen as the back door flew open and hit one of the cabinets. He was across the room, gun in his hand as the small figure shoved back the hood of her yellow rain slicker and took in the sight of the gun before turning to run back out the door.

Sebastian holstered his gun and caught her around her waist and hauled her back into the kitchen before she got more than one foot onto the back porch. She got in a good elbow to his ribs that made him grin.

Good for her.

"Calm down, I'm not going to hurt you," he said soothingly. Then he turned to his uncle who was standing in the middle of the kitchen looking like a dumbass.

"Armand, shut the damned door," Sebastian ordered.

Sebastian reared backwards as soon as he felt the woman in his arms get ready to headbutt him. "Whoa there, honey," he chuckled. He moved her to the middle of the kitchen and set her on her feet. She took a step backwards and looked between Sebastian and Armand.

"Armand, he hasn't hurt you has he?" Her voice was

breathy, as if she had just run a marathon.

"Don't mind my uncle, he's only staggering because he's drunk," Sebastian said as he looked over the woman standing in front of him. Despite the yellow rain jacket, her hair was still plastered to her head. All he could really tell about her was that she was short and her eyes were as stormy gray as the clouds outside.

She lifted an eyebrow as her gaze shifted toward Armand. "I thought we agreed you were going to go easy on the brandy, Armand?" It was a gentle reprimand.

Why does this woman, who's half the age of my drunken uncle, give a shit about him?

"Gee, it was just a little bit to help me sleep," he whined.

Sebastian's lip curled.

Gee's gaze turned to him.

"Gee?" Sebastian asked.

"Gianna Prentiss," she clarified as she began to unbutton her raincoat. "I'm renting the carriage house out back." As she removed her coat she smiled up at Sebastian then walked over to the cubby near the laundry room and hung up her jacket. She walked back to stand in front of him.

"So Armand is your uncle, huh? I've been here for six weeks now and nobody's mentioned you. What's your name?" Her smile was thoughtful.

Sebastian shook his head at his uncle in disgust. So much for Southern hospitality; all he was doing was eating up Gianna with his eyes, but hadn't bothered to even do any kind of basic introduction.

Asshat.

"It's nice to meet you, Gianna," Sebastian held out his hand. "I'm Sebastian Durand. I'm sorry I scared you."

"That's kind of an over-the-top reaction to somebody coming inside, isn't it? Are you a cop or something?" There was no fear in her voice, only curiosity, which piqued his. After greeting her with a gun and towering over her, Sebastian would have thought that Gianna would have had a little more trepidation when interacting with him, but she seemed fine in his presence.

Interesting.

It was also interesting that his grandfather was renting out the carriage house. Yeah, the old man might always be looking to line his coffers for the next election, but he sure as hell didn't need to be renting out the carriage house for cash. What the hell was up with this?

"Sebastian here is a war hero," Armand said in a sing-song voice, and Sebastian winced.

Gianna gave Sebastian a sideways look. "You're a veteran?" she asked.

"I'm active duty," he answered. "Navy."

She did a quick sweep of the kitchen and spied the plate on the table. "I'm assuming that's your dinner I'm interrupting, right?" she asked with a kind smile. "I came up here to remind Armand to eat; without Lazar here he sometimes loses track of time and forgets to eat dinner."

Armand stepped forward and put his arm around Gianna's shoulder. She stiffened, and a quick flash of distaste crossed her face before it morphed into a smile. "Gee here keeps me in line."

What the fuck?

Sebastian reached out and pulled Gianna's hand so that she was forced out of his Uncle's hold. "Why don't all three of us sit down and enjoy some of Ophelia's fried chicken?" he suggested. He tugged her with him toward the fridge. Satisfaction ran through his veins when he noted that she didn't stiffen up when she followed him. *Still, what kind of game is she playing?*

This is one fucked-up place.

3

Gianna studied the prodigal grandson from beneath her lashes as she took a bite of Ophelia's heavenly ambrosia salad. She knew that he'd left home to join the Navy when he was eighteen, and later became a Navy SEAL, but all of her research had said that he wasn't a part of the family anymore. She was going to have to call Jada and have her get some information on him…STAT.

"I can't pinpoint your accent, Gianna, where are you from?" Sebastian asked.

Damn, he's hot. How in the hell could Armand and Sebastian be related?

She finished chewing, then set down her fork. "Kentucky."

"Where in Kentucky?"

"Good luck finding answers, Gee doesn't like to tell much about herself," Armand said as he went back to the fridge. Gianna frowned when she saw him grab his third beer since sitting down. At this rate, he'd be passed out before sundown.

"Gianna?" Sebastian prompted.

"Oh." She turned back to see Sebastian's curious eyes. "It's a small town called Berea; all of my mother's family have lived there for generations."

"Now why does he get answers, and I don't, pretty girl?" Armand said as he stretched his arm over the back of her chair.

"You never specifically asked me what city I was from, Armand," she said with a small smile. She took another bite of chicken, thinking that if she could keep her mouth full she wouldn't have to answer any more questions. She picked up her glass of lemonade when Sebastian spoke again.

"So what brings you to our neck of the woods?"

"Work." She took a long sip. "Do you want seconds?" she looked down at his empty plate.

"What kind of work do you do?"

"I design textiles."

He frowned. "Want to run that by me again?"

"That takes more than a minute to explain. I'd really like to finish my meal."

"See?" Armand exclaimed. "She keeps her cards close to her vest."

She took a bite of her potato salad and watched as Sebastian gave his uncle an exasperated glance before getting up and taking his plate to the sink. He then opened the dishwasher, rinsed his plate and put it in, and started doing the same for the other dishes that cluttered the counter.

"Ophelia will take care of that when she gets back on Monday," Armand said with a wave of his hand.

Sebastian ignored him and continued with what he was doing.

When Gianna was finished, she took her dishes up to the counter, trying to figure out how she could help. He gave her a sideways glance. "I've got this," he said with an enticing smile.

"Can I help?"

"Sure, you can explain about designing textiles."

She sighed. "Textiles can be fabrics for clothing, bedding, furniture, and wallpaper. The kind of textile that you design for clothing is going to be different than what you would design for wallpaper."

"That makes sense," Sebastian said as he scraped off two days' worth of gunk from a plate. "So do you design for all types of media?"

Why did it take her by surprise that he used the word media? She gave him a fast glance out of the corner of her eye and he lifted an eyebrow. She'd been caught. He knew what she'd been thinking.

Blast it.

"It truly depends on what is inspiring me. I tend to design for bedding and clothing. I get my inspiration from the outdoors. It has done well for me." She started opening cupboards and drawers to see if she could find a washcloth that she could use to start wiping down the counter.

"What got you into this? Did you attend school to learn?"

"My granny was basically doing this with her quilting. My great aunt did amazing designs with her loom, and they both crocheted and knitted, then there was my granny's needle lace design. Both of them had nothing but boys, who had nothing but boys. When I came along, they crammed as much knowledge into me as they could."

"What's a loom?" Sebastian asked as Gianna found a washcloth and started cleaning the counter.

"It's a machine to weave. They were selling items throughout three counties."

"Were?"

"Aunt Ida is dead, and Granny's arthritis has forced her to stop. But she works in Tina's Treasures. It's one of the best stores that represents a lot of the local artists in Berea. Since Granny knows pretty much everybody in town, she can speak to all of the local artisans' works."

Gianna looked over her shoulder at Armand and saw that he wasn't paying any attention at all, he was thumbing off the label off his third or fourth beer.

"So you just grew up in the industry, no schooling?"

Gianna tipped her head to the side. "How about you answering some questions, Sebastian?"

"Why not?" He smiled as he put away the last dish into the dishwasher and closed it. He leaned back against the sink, crossing his arms and crossing his ankles.

Seeing the way his Henley shirt stretched over his broad chest, it took a moment for Gianna to gather her thoughts.

"What do you do in the Navy?"

"I'm with Navy Special Warfare," he answered.

"What does that mean?"

Sebastian shrugged. "It's like anything else in the military. It means I do whatever my lieutenant tells me to do."

"Okay, since you don't like that line of questioning, let's go for something else. What do you say?" Gianna relaxed when she saw his lips tip up.

"So how long are you going to be visiting?"

"Don't know. I have six weeks' leave available, but staying here the whole six weeks doesn't sound like a fun way to spend all of it," he said as he glanced over at his uncle.

She shifted and leaned her hip against the counter so she could get a better look at him. "Yeah, but it will be better when Lazar gets back from Baton Rouge, won't it?"

His expression darkened. "Oh, it'll get more interesting, that's for sure."

"Did you come here to see him, or Armand?"

"Oh, I came to see Grandpère. He said he'd be here now. I don't know why I'm surprised he's keeping me waiting."

"Maybe he was just caught at the capitol because of the hurricane," Gianna suggested.

Sebastian's mouth twisted. "Armand explained he had planned meetings there. Nope, this is just Lazar showing me that I'm here at his beck and call. I had forgotten how he ran things. Silly me."

Gianna contemplated his words. She hadn't seen that side of Lazar; he was always playing the perfect Southern gentleman with her. But she shouldn't be surprised—that was the reason she was here, wasn't it? It was to turn over the stones and see the sordid underbelly, and she knew darn good and well that Lazar's underbelly was sordid.

"How long has it been since you've been here for a visit?" she asked with a sweet smile. According to everything Jada had discovered, Sebastian had left home and never come back. In fact, when Gianna had made this trip, she'd never accounted for Sebastian to be any part of the situation.

"I haven't been home since I left at eighteen," he answered. She took note of him perusing her intently. "How did you come by renting out the carriage house? I know that occasionally my grandfather would have guests there, but never to my knowledge did he rent it out."

"It was really embarrassing how it came about," she said. "He found me trespassing, about six weeks ago. I had no idea that I was on private property," she lied, hoping he would buy into it.

"Why were you there?"

"I was sketching. It's kind of what I do." This time she was able to look him straight in his eye since it was the truth. "I get the ideas for a lot of my patterns from nature. I have spent years sketching the Appalachian mountains, but I saw some pictures of the bayou, and I fell in love."

"This is kind of out of the way, what made you pick this area?"

God, he has pretty eyes.

Gianna bit her lip. *Time for more lies.* "I wanted someplace really out of the way. No tourists, hopefully no people. I drove my Papaw's tent trailer out here and was staying in it when Neil ran across me."

Sebastian rubbed his chin and she could see he was trying to cover a grin. "Tent trailer? In hurricane season?"

"Granny and Pawpa have had it for decades and they've never had any problems with it," she said huffily. "Anyway, Neil found me parked under a shade tree near a river. I'd passed some boat launches about two miles back, and Neil explained that was a private launch that belonged to the Durand farm."

"So you didn't want complete privacy," Sebastian said with a smile.

"Knowing that there is a little bit of civilization is just good sense, for goodness sakes."

"Yes, it is."

"What are you two whispering about over there?" Armand asked as he shoved back his chair and weaved his way over to them. Sebastian had to steady him before he fell down.

"Armand, we're not whispering," Gianna smiled at him, then sighed. She felt both sad for him and disgusted. After weeks of talking to him, she'd realized just how privileged his life had been and how he'd squandered it away. The fact that he still felt that he'd been marginalized dumbfounded her, yet she knew he was hurting.

Armand shrugged out of Sebastian's hold and reached out for her. Gianna easily sidestepped him so that he ended up falling against the counter.

"What, now that Bastian's home, you're going to ignore me?" he glared at her.

"What are you talking about? We've talked about you drinking too much. You know I don't like to see you like this. I think you should go on up to bed." Gianna tried to keep her voice positive.

"Come give me a kiss goodnight." He held out his arms.

"No."

"Tomorrow night then, when I'm not drinking," he tried to cajole her.

Gianna hid her distaste. If she didn't need him so much, she wouldn't be putting up with this crud.

"Go to bed, Armand." She peeked over at Sebastian to see what he thought of all of this. She noticed that he was watching the interplay with intense concentration.

"I'll see you tomorrow, sweet thing," Armand said as he lurched toward the kitchen door leading to the hallway.

"Seems like you have an admirer," Sebastian said after the swinging door closed.

"He's harmless," Gianna said as she rinsed out the washcloth and hung it over the faucet to dry.

"Don't be so sure." Sebastian sounded serious.

She laughed up at him. "Trust me, I can take care of myself."

"Lady, you're barely five feet tall and all soft woman. I'm not seeing how you can take care of yourself if you're here alone with a drunk man who gets it in his head he wants something you don't want to give."

There was a definite bite in his tone.

"Did you not see the way he couldn't even walk? He'd trip over his own feet before he'd be able to catch me," Gianna said heatedly. "Anyway, he's harmless, and most times your grandfather and Ophelia are here. This whole conversation is moot."

Sebastian didn't respond, he just stared down at her from his lofty height. Now *here* was a dangerous man. If *he* wanted to take advantage of her, there would be no stopping him.

His gaze softened and he slowly smiled. "I would never hurt you, or any woman."

Gianna nodded.

"I can get you some letters of recommendation if you'd like. I'd start with Ophelia, then there is my friend Braxton's mom and his four sisters, they'd write letters. I could also get my next-door neighbor, Mrs. Crabtree, to write a letter. She really likes me because I mow her grass when I'm in town."

Gianna couldn't stop her smile. "How old is Mrs. Crabtree?"

"She's eighty if she's a day, but that doesn't stop her from talking about my ass."

"What?!"

"Swear to God. She told me that her great-niece would really like me because I'm kind and that I have a great ass. I almost spit out the sweet tea that she'd made for me. But if you ever tell anybody that I told you, I'll deny it."

Sebastian's eyes danced with mirth, and now Gianna thought his eyes were spectacular.

"I really want to read her letter of recommendation. However, I wonder if she would give you one, seeing as how she probably wants you for her great-niece."

"Well, there is that," Sebastian agrees with a grin. "I saw pie in the fridge, want some?"

"Nah, I'm full. I need to get back to the carriage house."

"I'll walk you back," Sebastian said.

Gianna looked out the window at the wind and rain. "No, you won't. There's no reason for us both to get soaked. Stay here, I'll be fine."

She headed for the coat rack and Sebastian followed her. He reached over her head and grabbed his jacket when she grabbed hers.

"I'm serious, Sebastian. I don't need you walking me the few yards it takes to get to the cottage."

"Okay." He nodded. He helped her put on her coat, then put his on. She walked to the back door and he opened it for her. When she stepped out onto the porch, he put his arm around her shoulder.

"You're not going to listen to me, are you?" She had to shout to be heard above the wind and rain.

"Nope."

He kept her close as they walked down the gravel path and around to the front of the carriage house. When they got under the overhang, she pushed open the door.

"You didn't lock it?" he asked as they got inside.

"Of course not," she said as she took off her coat and hung it up.

"Gianna, you always need to lock your door."

"I never have to lock my door here, nobody lives here. It's fine."

Sebastian stepped forward with a hard look on his face. His hands came up and captured her face. "You never fuck around with your safety. Ever. Never. You got me?"

His expression was intense. Beyond intense. Freaked.

"Okay, Sebastian, I'll lock my door, I promise," she whispered.

Then, as if he noticed what he'd done, he stepped back.

"Okay, good." Sebastian walked over to the window, then shook his head. "Shit, there are no hurricane shutters."

"What are hurricane shutters?"

"Helen is gaining strength and due to hit New Orleans tonight. I can't believe Neil hasn't installed hurricane shutters on this place. You're going to need to stay the night in the big house. Pack a bag."

"What are you talking about?"

Sebastian motioned for her to follow him to the window that faced the big house. "There, see how all of the windows on the second and third floors have closed shutters over them? Those are hurricane shutters that Neil must have closed before he and Ophelia went home. Armand should have already shut the ones on the first floor." Sebastian shook his head with disgust.

Gianna saw the pretty green shutters covering all of the windows. She'd noticed them before, and thought they were just for decoration.

"They don't really get hurricanes where I live. We occasionally get a tornado every now and then, but those are few and far between." Gianna bit her lip. "How bad is this going to get?"

"It was only a Cat Four in Georgia, but it went south into the Gulf of Mexico and gained speed and is now heading our way. I'm hearing it could be a Cat Five by the time it lands. It's not good. Now pack a bag, and I'll get the shutters closed on the first floor when we get back to the house."

"Okay."

4

When Sebastian went out to the tool shed, he found there was a combination lock on it.

"Dammit," he grimaced, as he ran back to the house. He needed the power drill so that he could lock down the shutters. When he went into Armand's room to find out if he knew the combination, the sorry bastard had no idea.

"Didn't Neil give you the combination before he left?" Sebastian asked. "Weren't you supposed to close up the shutters on the first floor?"

Armand lifted himself up on his elbow and frowned. "I can't remember. I think so. Don't need to, though. Neil always worries too much." He flopped back down onto the mattress.

"What is the combination to the shed?" Sebastian asked again.

"Go away."

Sebastian slammed Armand's bedroom door shut, then went downstairs. He grabbed his phone to call Lazar; maybe he'd have Neil's phone number, because sure as shit, his grandfather wouldn't have the combination. His call went to voicemail.

"Dammit."

Sebastian headed to the kitchen, hoping that there would be a screwdriver in the junk drawer. Gianna was there, mixing something in a bowl. He opened the drawer that he remembered that housed a lot of miscellaneous shit and started to dig through it.

"What are you looking for?" she asked.

"Need to lock down the shutters. Would like to use the power drill, but don't know the combination to the shed."

"Won't Neil know?" Gianna asked.

"Sure." He nodded as he sifted through pencils, pens, gum, decks of cards, and matches.

"I have Ophelia's number."

Sebastian's head jerked up. "Well hell, I should have thought to ask you. Can you give it to me?" he asked as he pulled out his cell phone.

Gianna laughed.

"I don't have it memorized. Come with me and I'll get my cell."

They left the kitchen and Sebastian waited at the bottom of the stairs as Gianna ran upstairs to get her phone.

He tried not to be too obvious as he watched her breasts bounce as she ran down the stairs to hand him her phone. "Just call from mine," she said as she handed him her cell.

"Thanks." He pressed the contact for Ophelia.

"Hey, Gianna, how are you holding up? Did you like the ambrosia salad I made for you?"

The sound of Ophelia's voice hit Sebastian like a ton of bricks. He hadn't realized just how much he had missed her until that very moment.

"Hi, Philly," he whispered.

"Sebastian? Is that you?" Her voice was a mere whisper.

"Yeah."

"My God, boy. Oh my God. Talk some more. Say something for me, baby."

"Gonna cook some of my favorite foods while I'm here?" he asked, trying to put a smile in his voice.

"Ophelia, are you okay?"

Sebastian heard Neil speaking in the background.

"I'm fine, I'm fine. Don't bother me. I'm talking to Sebastian. Hush up."

"Sebastian? Let me talk to the boy." Neil bellowed.

"Old man, I told you to hush up." There was the sound of rustling, then Ophelia spoke again. "My boy. Are you home? How long are you going to stay? Are you all right? Why are you home?"

Sebastian chuckled. "One question at a time, Philly." He watched as Gianna walked down the hall, most likely to give him some privacy.

"You can handle it. Now answer me."

He could hear the tears in her voice and it was gutting him. Fuck, why hadn't he kept in touch with her?

"I'm here at the house. I'm going to be staying at least a couple of weeks. I'm fine, absolutely fine. Grandpère asked me to come home. We have some unfinished business."

He was met by silence.

"Is this a good idea?"

Ophelia knew more than almost anybody in the world about Sebastian's life. She knew the hurt and pain he'd suffered in this house.

"It's been years Philly. It's time."

She blew out a long breath. "Lazar isn't due home for a couple of days. I'll make sure to be there when he gets home."

Sebastian's smile got even bigger. Absolutely nothing had changed; Ophelia was still trying to be his protector.

"I'm a big boy now, Philly. Gianna told me you're spending time with your grandkids. You take your time. I'm just calling because I need your loving husband's combination to the shed. I need to get the drill to get the shutters locked down."

"Hold on, let me get him." There was a pause. "I love you, sweet boy."

There it was, another shot to his heart.

"Love you too, Philly."

"Neil! Sebastian needs you. Get your butt over here."

Sebastian grinned. Some things never changed.

"Whatchya need boy?" Another voice that he'd missed.

"I need the combination to the shed," Sebastian said.

"What in God's name do you need that for? You should be hunkering down. The hurricane is about to hit."

"I know that. Gotta get the shutters locked down. Need the combination so I can get to your tools."

"Armand should have done that already. Told him what to do. I handed him the damn drill, God knows where he put it. Made sure he was sober at the time."

Sebastian rubbed the back of his neck. "My fault, Neil. What in the hell was I thinking? I asked for the combination for the shed so I could lock down the shutters—never occurred to me that he had the drill."

"Dumb son of a bitch should have known what you needed. Jesus, that man has never had a lick of sense."

"Ain't that the truth? I'll go wake him up and ask him where he put it."

"You do that. Good to have you back, boy. I want to hear what all you've been up to when Ophelia and I get back, so make sure you set aside some time for me."

"Will do."

"Wanna talk to Ophelia again?" Neil asked.

"Nah, gotta get the shutters locked down. I'll see you soon enough, but don't let her cut her visit short, I'm going to be here for two weeks."

"I won't. She loves spoiling our grandbabies. Bye, Son."

"Goodbye, Neil."

Sebastian ended the call, then went looking for Gianna. He found her at the back of the house, in the sunroom, she was in one of the rocking chairs, studying one of the old coffee table books that Lazar had lying around the house.

"Brought back your phone," Sebastian said as he handed it to her.

She smiled as she took it.

"You didn't have to leave," he said.

"Oh, okay."

Sebastian got the feeling that she would leave in the future too. Somebody had taught her courtesy. She hadn't talked about her mother; he wondered what she was like.

"Did you find out the combination?"

Sebastian grimaced. "Don't need it. Armand has the drill somewhere in the house. Neil gave it to him. Gotta go wake him up again," Sebastian said with disgust.

"Again?"

"I already woke him up once to ask him the combination. Dumbass should have known I needed the drill."

Gianna's lips twitched.

This was definitely a mystery; why in the hell was she cozying up to a man who was a drunk and a fool? Well, he didn't have time to figure this shit out now, he needed to get the shutters closed. He'd have plenty of time to work on that tomorrow. In the meantime, he'd focus on trying to get his uncle to remember *what* in the hell a drill *was*, let alone *where* it was.

"Are you safe?" Jada asked.

"I'm fine," Gianna assured her friend over their video call on her computer. She pulled up the extra blankets so that her legs were covered, and was happy that she was wearing her hoodie. It was warm and humid, but there was something about the sound of wind and rain that made her feel cold.

"Seriously, babe, I'm hearing this could turn into a Category Five hurricane, and you're in the middle of bumfuck Louisiana with the drunk, handsy-assed clown. Are. You. Safe?"

Gianna snickered as she turned down the volume on her computer. She would've worn her headphones, but then she'd have no idea how loud she was, and Jada had a tendency to make her laugh really loud.

"Turn up your volume, because I'm going to whisper," she told her best friend.

"What, are you telling me that the boozed-up Cajun isn't passed out tonight and might actually hear us? Or does the Crypt Creeper have his hearing aids in?"

Gianna giggled even louder. "You gotta stop making me laugh, Sebastian will hear me." Then her head whipped up as she heard another piercing howl of wind coming from behind the shuttered windows. "Scratch that, nobody's going to hear anything above the wind."

"That goes back to my original question. Are you safe?"

"Yeah, I'm fine. Sebastian made me come stay at the big house when he realized that the carriage house didn't have storm shutters."

Jada's brown eyes got wide. "Sebastian is there? As in Navy SEAL Sebastian Lazar Durand the Fourth?"

"That'd be the one," Gianna confirmed.

"Holy shit. What is he doing there? According to everything I sourced he left at eighteen and has never shown back up."

"You're my information guru, go find out."

Jada shook her head, her curls bouncing. "I will get you everything you need, you know that, after you answer my damned question. Are you safe?"

"Oh my God. You are not my keeper," Gianna glared at her computer screen.

"Gianna, you're a babe in the woods. If you hadn't had me to take care of you at New York University you would have been eaten alive. Damn good thing you got me as your roommate our freshman year."

Gianna rolled her eyes in protest, but Jada was speaking the absolute truth. She might have lived the first four-and-a-half years of her life surrounded by pimps, drugs, and whores, but after that, she'd been a sheltered girl who had lived in a small Kentucky town surrounded by grandparents who did everything they could to shield her from all of life's harshness. They'd hated it when she'd received a scholarship to NYU, but in the end, they had supported her choice to follow her dream.

"I'm safe. I'm safe. You'd think that Sebastian was some kind of broody hen and I was one of his baby chicks. He couldn't get my butt up to the big house fast enough. Then he threw a fit because the storm shutters weren't locked down on the first floor on this house, and he was going to go out there in the middle of the storm with a darned screwdriver to secure them." Gianna gave her friend the 'eek' face.

"You're freaking kidding me."

"I told him I had Ophelia's number so he could get ahold of Neil; that way he could get into the toolshed and get the drill. Then he was sooo darned sweet." Gianna bit her lip and sighed.

"Well, don't leave me hanging; how was he sweet?"

"He called Ophelia, Philly, and his voice was so soft and caring, it made my heart melt."

"What all did he say to her?" Jada demanded to know.

"I don't know. I left the room to give them some privacy.

"Didn't you eavesdrop? Tell me you eavesdropped. I would have."

"You would not have."

"You know I would have."

Gianna laughed. It was so true, Jada would totally have listened in on the conversation.

"All I know is that when he was done, he stormed into Armand's room and rousted him out of bed and made him go room by room until the fool could put his hands on the drill. Apparently, Neil had given it to him before he had left. God knows why, I can't believe Neil thought that Armand was going to actually lock the shutters down on the first floor. The man is useless."

Jada threw back her head and laughed. "That had to have been a sight to see. Did you manage not to laugh?"

"For real, I actually drew blood because I bit my lip so hard. But..."

Jada stared at her, cocking her head to the side, and waited. When Gianna didn't say anything for over a minute, she finally prodded.

"But what?"

"There's something about Sebastian. I can't explain it."

A slow grin spread over Jada's face. "Describe him to me. Is he one of those hot blonde white boys?"

Gianna shook her head. "He's tall. At least six foot two. He had dark scruff and longer hair than I would have expected for a military man. His jaw was square and he has the thickest eyelashes I've ever seen on a man."

"Jesus." Jada leaned back against her headboard. "What color are his eyes?"

"Green, but not like emerald green. They're more like the color of sea glass."

"What about his body? It has to be good, what with him being a Navy SEAL and all."

"He was wearing a Henley and it was tight. His muscles had muscles. Seriously, Jada, I might have had a spontaneous orgasm when I saw him take off his jacket."

"I have got to come visit. Do you think the Lazar could handle a smart-mouthed, brown girl from Queens?"

"How could he not love my best friend? But I call dibs on Sebastian," Gianna said in a teasing voice.

"I kind of caught that, honey." Jada smiled. "Now, for the important stuff. I've come up with something interesting on Armand. I don't know if it is anything, but it might pertain."

"Hit me." Gianna relaxed against the pillows she had piled behind her.

"You know that Sebastian Lazar Durand the Third was the old man's golden boy. He was supposed to follow his daddy's footsteps into politics. I figured it would be smart to check into Armand and see what he was doing around the time of Number Three's death, and this is where the fun begins."

Jada stopped herself. "Fuck, did I just say that? I'm sorry, there is nothing fun about how your hottie's dad died. Anyway, four years before Number Three died Armand drew a significant amount of money out of his trust fund. I knew the money went to some bogus LLC out of Delaware, but that means nothing; most LLCs in

America operate out of Delaware. It took some digging, but it is the shell company for the Leather Library Gentlemen's Club outside of Baton Rouge. That place is known for their high-end VIP cigar rooms, where most of the Louisiana state legislature will shell out ten grand for a bottle of booze, served to them by damn near-naked women."

"Shoot," Gianna drawled out. "It seems like everything revolves around sex. Do you think my mother ever worked there?"

"As far as I can tell, there was never any sex involved there. Instead, that place was used more for private meetings amongst the high-end political players of Louisiana. As for your mom working there? I don't think so. But I do think that the clientele at the Leather Library were the same clients that Etta Rose had."

"So basically, they were Mom's clients," Gianna whispered softly.

"That's my two cents," Jada agreed.

"But we already knew that, so why do we care if Armand has a stake in this club?"

"Armand has been useless since day one. Who he is today is who he was back then. He never mattered to his father, and we know this because he was never brought into the family business of politics. Instead, he was supposed to be in charge of the family farm, and even that he couldn't hack. So I'm saying it's pretty strange that at thirty-five he starts investing in a shady gentlemen's club? Something isn't adding up," Jada insisted.

"Jada, I understand this new information about Armand is interesting, but I'm here to find out how my mom went from being one of Etta's girls to a strung-out addict working the streets. You and I agreed that our best bet was tracking down known customers of Etta's, or some of the other call girls she worked with. Or best yet, Etta Rose herself."

"And that's what you're doing, Babe. According to that one call girl you interviewed, Lazar was one of the biggest customers back in the day, and he would throw big parties and hire out a dozen girls at a time. He's still your best bet."

"Well, okay then. I agree. And I have a plan."

"Does it have something to do with you staying at the big house with Lazar out of town?"

"You know me so well." Gianna grinned. "Lazar's office is on the ground floor, and with the wind howling like it is, not even a Navy SEAL will hear me when I go sleuthing."

"Whoa there, Nancy Drew, what do you expect to find?"

"I'm thinking that Lazar is old. Really old. Crypt Creeper is old. So I would bet my bottom dollar he has paper files. I have no idea what I'm looking for exactly, but I'm going to give this a shot. Tonight's when Hurricane Helen is supposed to hit full force, so I'm going to take full advantage."

"Is your phone charged?"

Gianna looked over to where her phone was plugged into the charger. "It's charging now."

"Girly, pick it up and tell me what percentage the charge is; you always run it down to less than ten percent."

Gianna rolled her eyes and reached for it. "It's at seventy-eight, smart-aleck."

"You really need to learn how to swear. Okay, seventy-eight is good. I want you to take the phone with you, call me, and then keep it on mute. I want to be able to hear everything."

"What good will that do? You going to call the cops and say, 'Hi, I know it's the middle of a hurricane, but my friend was just caught trespassing through somebody's office, can you send help?' Yeah, that sounds good."

Jada bit one of her pared-down nails. "Fine, smartass, just Skype me when you're done."

"You'll be asleep."

"You better fucking Skype me, or I'll fucking kick your ass!"

Gianna giggled. "Yes, Mom, I will. And don't forget to do your part of the job. Find out everything you can on the hot SEAL."

"You know what would help me with that research?" Jada asked.

"What?"

"Naked pictures."

"Good night, Jada."

5

Gianna used her phone's flashlight to make it downstairs to the kitchen and grabbed the screwdriver that Sebastian had returned to the junk drawer, then headed for Lazar's study. When she got there, she closed the door and turned on his two desk lamps. His study was huge; when she really looked around she realized it must have been another living room or drawing room at some point, and Lazar had turned it into his office. Figured. The man had an outsized ego, so he needed a humongous office that would fit his head.

She went around the desk and sat down in the old leather chair. It creaked with age. The desk didn't have any kind of paperwork on it, just a leather blotter and four pictures in overly ornate frames. She already knew who everyone was because Lazar had told her. One was a picture of Lazar's parents on their wedding day. That would be Sebastian Lazar Durand the First and his wife. They looked so stiff and solemn. Gianna hoped, for their sakes, that it wasn't a precursor to things to come. Then there was a picture of Lazar and his wife Lorraine Beauregard, the typical Southern Belle. Lazar had told her all about Lorraine; that is to say, all about her bloodlines as if she were some kind of prized heifer that he had purchased. When Gianna had asked what she was like, what kind of mother she'd been or how she'd spent her days, Lazar had looked like Gianna was crazy. Just another reason she'd come to despise the old man.

The next picture was of Sebastian the Third. No wedding photo for him—he'd gotten a divorce, so his wife didn't deserve any kind of remembrance. Jada had provided a lot of information about his murdered wife Pamela, including a picture. She had been a beautiful woman, both inside and out.

The last picture was of Sebastian the Fourth. It was his high school graduation photo, and he looked so young and solemn. She could see hints of the man he was to become, but life had definitely hardened him. She reached out and stroked his face.

"What happened to you?" she wondered.

Enough of this. She needed to get to work. She started to open drawers. Most of them were unlocked. They were mostly empty. She found cough drops, stamps, envelopes, paperclips.

"Ewww..."

She snatched her hand back when she realized she'd touched a treasure trove of used tissues. Seriously, he had a trashcan underneath his desk. Then there was the flask. On the right-hand side of the desk was a locked drawer. She looked at the screwdriver that was resting on top of the desk. If she used it, it would be pretty darned obvious that Lazar's desk had been broken into. How could she explain that?

She took her phone off mute. "Jada."

"What?"

"Can you google how to pick a lock? I have a screw-driver and could force the desk drawers open, but that would be kind of obvious."

Jada sighed. "Facetime me so I can see the kind of lock we're dealing with."

Gianna pressed the Facetime button and pointed the phone at the lock.

"Come on, Girly, I need light."

"I don't want to turn on the overhead lights. It's bad enough that I have the desk lights on," Gianna complained.

"Do you want me to do this, or not?"

Gianna huffed and marched over to the door and slammed the switch to turn on the overhead lights. Then she went back to the desk and squatted down.

"Now can you see?"

"Yes, that's much better. Shit, how old is this desk anyway?"

"How should I know? Old."

"Okay, I'm googling. Are there other file cabinets that you could be looking at in the meantime?" Jada asked.

Giana turned on her heels and peered around the chair. "Yeah. But do you need me to still hold the phone?"

"Nah. Just put the phone down while I do the search. I'll holler when I've got something, you go look around."

Gianna turned around to the credenza and found the drawers locked, but the cupboards were unlocked. She sat down cross-legged in front of them, then started pulling out manila file folders. She'd been right—he was old-school, the man was totally into paper files.

The first dozen were all about household accounts, which were useless. Then she found one titled Ophelia, and she found papers dating back thirty-two years.

"You cheap lint-licker!"

"What did you say?" Jada yelled through the phone.

She crawled over to the desk and grabbed the phone, then went back to the credenza. "I just found all of the files on Ophelia and a bunch of cashed checks. Not only is Lazar a lech, he's robbing Ophelia!"

"Calm down," Jada demanded. "What are you talking about?"

"I just found out what he's paying her. It's not even minimum wage, and he has her on salary, and I know that she works more than forty hours a week."

"You've got to be shitting me."

"I'm not."

Gianna threw down the file and grabbed the one that said Neil on it. With him, she found a letter written three years ago that looked like some bogus employment contract, that showed him getting a fifty-cent raise. It went on to state the original terms of employment which stated no paid vacation, five paid holidays, and no health insurance. Gianna felt her eyes begin to burn with tears.

She explained to Jada everything she read. "That's not legal, is it? He has to provide health insurance, right?"

"No honey, small employers don't," Jada whispered.

"Why didn't they quit?"

"I don't know what kind of jobs are available there in that little town."

"But Lazar has a lot of money, you hacked his bank accounts! He's a cheap, stinking, gnarled, skeezy, lint-licker!"

"Yes, he is," Jada said soothingly. "But this isn't what we're after. You need to keep on track, okay? We need information that will help us find your mom. If we can find something on him that will help us blackmail him so he will tell us what he might know about your mom, or any information on Etta Rose, then we're golden."

Gianna wiped away her tears on the sleeve of her hoodie.

"You're right. Did you find anything to help break into the desk drawers?"

"Yeah, I'm going to need you to crawl under the desk and find out the maker's mark. It should be listed on a brass plate."

Gianna stuffed the files that she had gone through back into the credenza and started to crawl back to the desk. At least the office was carpeted.

When she got under the desk, she couldn't see anything. It was too dark. "Hey, Jada, I'm going to have to call you back. I need to turn on my phone's flashlight to see anything under here, and I don't know how to operate two functions at once."

"You could use my phone," a low voice rumbled.

Gianna screamed, jerked up, and slammed her head on the bottom of the desk.

"Owwww," she cried. She fell onto the floor in pain.

"What the fuck is happening?" Jada screeched.

Gianna curled up into the fetal position and squealed when a warm hand gently touched her back.

"Calm down, honey, I didn't mean to scare you. It's me, Sebastian. I need to see how badly you hurt yourself."

Gianna whimpered and reached around to the back of her head. It felt hot and she could swear she already feel a lump forming.

"Can I help you out from underneath there?"

"Sebastian, what's wrong with Gianna?" Jada demanded to know.

His touch was tender as he drew her out from under the desk. Gianna looked up into his concerned eyes. "Can you sit up?"

She nodded, then regretted it. "I'm fine," she said as she

pushed herself up into a seated position then slumped back against the desk.

"Would somebody tell me what the fuck is going on?" Jada yelled.

Gianna closed her eyes, knowing she was in a ton of trouble.

"Your partner in crime smacked her head on the bottom of the desk. I'm trying to see how bad it is."

"Do you have any medical training, SEAL boy?"

Gianna gulped. She didn't feel well and Jada wasn't helping.

"Yes," Sebastian said. "I'm going to hang up now. Gianna can call you back when she's feeling better."

"Whoa there. My girl is hurting. I need to know you're not going to give her a bunch of shit for being in the office."

"Scout's Honor. I'm not going to give her shit."

"Were you a Boy Scout?" Jada demanded to know.

"Fuck no. Now goodbye."

Gianna opened her right eye to see how mad Sebastian was.

"Can you open both eyes?" he asked softly.

"Depends. On a scale of one to ten, how angry are you going to be if I'm able to open both eyes?" she asked.

"Ten for hurting yourself, one for snooping."

Gianna opened her left eye. Sebastian didn't look angry. His large hands lifted and reached around her head to tenderly probe her scalp. He winced when she did. "Come on, sweetheart, let's get you to the office couch, then I'll get some ice from the kitchen."

Gianna had to lean against him in order to make her way over to the leather couch. When she started to lie down, she crinkled her nose when the smell of brandy and cigarette smoke hit her nostrils.

"What is it?"

"Armand must have spilled his drink on the sofa."

Sebastian leaned down and took a deep breath. "Jesus."

He picked her up and she squeaked. "What are you doing?"

"We'll go out to the drawing-room. That couch is more comfortable anyway, along with the added bonus of not stinking."

Gianna was shocked. She had never been carried in her whole life. At least not that she remembered. She'd been almost five when her grandparents came and rescued her, too old to be carried, and God knows that neither her dad nor mom had ever picked her up.

"Honey, relax. You're stiff as a board. Put your arms around my neck."

She looked up into Sebastian's eyes and they were warm. As if a switch had been flipped, her entire body melted into his hold.

"That's better, now put your arms around my neck."

She did. Sebastian bent down a little bit to open the door to the office, then it felt like she was flying through the air as he strode down the hall to the drawing-room. Ever so gently he placed her onto the sofa, making sure that the back of her head didn't hit the cushions.

"I'll be right back with some ice, pillows, and a blanket. Here you go." He reached into his back pocket and handed her her phone.

"You remembered this?" How could he have remembered her phone? She hadn't even remembered her phone.

"Of course. Now call your girl and tell her what's going on. She seemed freaked."

"Okay."

Sebastian left the room.

Gianna looked at her phone but she was too tired to hit Jada's number.

This was not good.

"Gianna, can you wake up for me?" Sebastian gave her shoulder a gentle shake.

"Huh?" Her eyelashes fluttered, but she didn't open her eyes.

"Honey, I need you to open your eyes."

"Wanna sleep."

Sebastian lifted her head and put two pillows underneath her. Then he positioned her so that he could place the bag of frozen peas so that it rested between the bump on her head and the back of the sofa.

Her eyes slammed open. "Cold!"

Sebastian chuckled. "It's supposed to be cold."

Gianna lifted her hand to the frozen bag, but Sebastian caught her before she could pull it away. "Stop that, Champ, you need to keep the ice on to stop the swelling."

"Not a champ. Didn't play sports," she scowled. "Don't like sports."

Sebastian chuckled again. Her scowl was cute.

When she moved her head away from the ice, he gently pushed her back against it. Her hand slapped against his. "Stop that. I told you it was cold!"

Sebastian really started to laugh.

"And stop laughing at me."

"Then stop being funny."

Gianna tried to sit up before he could stop her, then she groaned. "That hurts." Sebastian helped her to lie back down.

"Honey, do you remember hitting your head?"

She frowned. Then her eyes went really wide. "Oh frick. You apprehended me!"

Yep, funnier than shit. "Actually, I think I was offering you the use of my flashlight."

He watched as she considered what he said. "You're right, you did." A slow grin spread over her face. "Plus, you're being pretty darned nice to me right now. What's up with that?"

"Hmmm, there's a lot of possibilities. How about the whole Southern hospitality thing?"

Gianna looked at him carefully. "Yeah, I don't think that's it. Try another one."

"I thought you were cleaning underneath my grandfather's desk and you needed more light?"

Gianna snickered. "Nope. Try again."

"You're beautiful and I want to ingratiate myself with you?"

Gianna snorted with laughter, then winced, her hand going to the back of her head. "Darn, that really hurts."

It was cute how she didn't swear. You really didn't see that anymore.

"So tell me why you offered the flashlight."

"I will after you tell me what you were looking for in Lazar's office."

She bit her bottom lip. "I really can't."

"You mean you won't."

Her phone rang. Sebastian saw the name Jada Harlow appear on the screen. "Didn't you call back Jada?"

"I was too tired. Shoot, I probably really worried her." She swiped her phone. "I'm sorry Jada, I'm fine. I promise. Sebastian put ice on my head and it's cold. He gave me pillows. He says he's not apprehending me, instead he tried to make me guess why he tried to help, but now he wants to know what I was looking for in the office and I don't know what to tell him."

"Breathe, Baby," her friend whispered.

Gianna closed her eyes. When she opened them again, Sebastian saw she had her shit together, and that she was once more like the woman he had met in the kitchen.

"Got it." Her eyes slid over to look at Sebastian. "What were you doing in Lazar's office in the middle of the night?" she asked him.

"Wondered when you were going to ask me that," he said with a grin.

"Well, I'm pretty sure that even with your secret SEAL senses you couldn't have heard me come downstairs with the wind howling like it is."

That stopped him short. "That's twice you two have mentioned me being a SEAL. Wanna tell me what's going on?" he asked quietly.

Gianna's eyes went wide. "Shoot, Jada, I'll call you back. Seems I stepped in it." She ended the call.

"Yep, you stepped in it. Textiles huh?"

Gianna attempted to push up into a sitting position, but Sebastian pushed her back down on the couch. She glared up at him. "SEAL, huh?"

"Yep. Plus, I'm the one who actually is a member of this family, so it's my prerogative to check out every room in the house. You, however, aren't. So how about you tell me what in the hell you and your little friend were looking for in Lazar's office?"

"Answers," she said succinctly.

That hit him like a punch to his solar plexus. How many years had he been after answers? Wasn't that the reason he had been planning to go through his grandfather's office tonight?

"What questions do you need answers for?"

"That's none of your business." Her expression was determined.

Sebastian needed to try a different tack. Remembering what he'd heard the two women talking about he tried again. "Who is Etta Rose?"

"She was a madam. She ran a really exclusive escort service years ago."

Well, he sure as hell wasn't expecting that.

"And why do you think you're going to find information on Etta Rose in my grandfather's office?"

Gianna huffed out a breath and her eyes narrowed. "It's a long story."

Sebastian put his right hand on the back of the sofa and leaned in. "Well, aren't we lucky? I've got the rest of the night for you to tell me a bedtime story. So talk."

"Etta Rose used to run a service out of New Orleans. She would recruit young women from the universities there, like Loyola and Tulane. The girls would make good coin and end up graduating free of debt."

"Are we talking escorts or prostitutes or both?"

"I know that there was sex involved," Gianna said slowly.

"I take it since you're investigating dear old Grandpère I should assume that her business encompassed Baton Rouge?"

"Oh yeah. From what Jada and I have been able to piece together, the members of the state legislature were big-time customers."

"So what does this have to do with you?"

"Why do you think this has anything to do with me?" she asked.

Sebastian looked at her. If she could have, she would be crossing her arms across her chest, or curled into a defensive ball. He'd been wondering why she'd been sucking up to his uncle when he could sense her distaste. Then there had been moments of real concern about whether he'd eaten. Now it was all making sense. Gianna was a marshmallow. It was obvious as hell that she had some kind of personal stake in whatever she was investigating. Something overwhelmingly personal. Now all he had to do was get her to tell him what it was.

"Talk to me Gianna, maybe I can help."

"Look, nobody's heard from Etta Rose for at least fifteen years, so what makes you think this has anything to do with me? I'm just trying to track down some old information."

Her gaze slid sideways to look at the far wall. Sebastian growled with frustration. "Fine, it has nothing to do with you."

Gianna flinched, and Sebastian sighed. "Look, just get some rest and keep the ice on your head. I'll come back and check on you, okay?"

Her lashes fluttered shut. "Okay," she murmured.

What in the hell was going on?

6

It was only zero four hundred in Virginia; it would be a pretty shitty thing to do to call Gideon at this hour. Still, he could shoot him a text to have him call him when he got his ass out of bed. Sebastian sent the text before he went upstairs to his room, then he rifled through his duffel bag. He grinned when he found what he was looking through in his Dopp kit. Landon would be so proud that he was finally using the birthday gift that he'd given him.

Sebastian peeked in on Gianna and saw that she was still sleeping before heading back to his grandfather's office. The desk and credenza were old and all had pin tumbler locks. He unfolded the leather billfold with the lock-pick tools and pulled out the snake rake tool. It took less than thirty seconds to unlock the first drawer.

"Damn, Granddad, just how old are these files?"

Sebastian tried not to sneeze as he pulled out the discolored manila file folders. He set them on the desk. When he got all of them up on the desk, he pulled the drawer out even farther, not all that surprised to see that there were more papers stuffed farther in the back. Lazar was nothing if not predictable. He pulled out those crinkled papers as well, he'd save those for last.

Each file folder had a man's name on it. He only recognized four names, all the rest meant nothing to him, so he had to google the others on his phone. Almost all of them had at one time been associated with the Louisiana state government, or they were extremely wealthy Louisiana businessmen.

"Let's see what's inside."

Sebastian started with a name he recognized. The man was now head of the National Environmental Protection Agency. Turned out he'd started out as a lowly state senator in Louisiana about the time that his dear old grandfather had started his political career.

There were a lot of letters going back and forth between the two men, all perfectly above-board, mostly ass-kissing types about how they would support one another on upcoming pieces of legislation. Sebastian quickly flipped through the remaining pages and saw nothing but the same thing. Then he went onto the next file of a name he recognized. Same thing.

By the time he was done with the thirty files, he found nothing. Not one damn thing. He rubbed the back of his neck, trying to alleviate the headache he felt building. Shit, he needed to go check on Gianna. He glanced at his watch. An hour and a half had passed since he'd sat down. When he went down the hall towards the drawing-room, it sounded like he was in a wind tunnel. The hurricane had to be right on top of them.

Gianna was still asleep. He crouched down in front of the sofa; the fact that she was sleeping through such loud noise was worrisome.

"Hey, Beautiful, can you open your eyes?"

"Go away." she slurred.

"Gianna, I need you to look at me," he said a little louder. He tucked a lock of her dark hair behind her ear.

Her eyes opened. "Not you again." Sebastian grinned at her surly attitude.

"'Fraid so. How's your head feel?"

She scrunched her brow. "Depends. Is there a lot of noise in the house, or have Irish river dancers decided to use my head as their new stage?"

Sebastian threw back his head and laughed.

"Stop that," she grumbled. "I don't need more noise, it hurts."

"Are you always such a complainer?"

"You're the one who injured me. So my complaining is your fault, so you just have to deal with it." Her eyes narrowed. "And another thing. If you didn't want me to complain, you shouldn't have woken me up."

"If you weren't so damned funny, you would be pretty damned annoying, you know that?"

"That's what Jada always says too." Gianna pushed at the blanket and sat up before Sebastian had a chance to stop her.

"You need to lie back down."

"Nope, done with the invalid portion of the evening," she said as she put both of her hands up to press against her temples.

"I'm serious, just go back to sleep."

She put her hands down in her lap, her expression calm. "And I'm serious too, Sebastian, I'm fine. The ice helped, so I'm going to bed."

Her pupils were dilated, and there were white lines of strain around her mouth. She was hurting.

"I'm going to get you some ibuprofen and more ice, and you're going to lay your happy ass back down on the couch," he grumbled.

"Do these caveman tactics work much?" When she went to swing her legs off the couch, he stopped her.

"Gianna, here's how it's going to be. You go up to your room, I'm still going to come in and check on you every couple of hours. You have a nasty bump, and I want to make sure you're all right, so what's it going to be? Down here, or upstairs?"

She glared at him. "Fine. I'll stay down here."

He choked back a laugh. "I'll go get you a glass of water and some ibuprofen."

He was almost out of the room when heard, "Quit being so annoyingly nice."

"You're welcome."

Gideon called him while he was getting the medicine for Gianna.

"I'll call you right back."

"Whatever works," Gideon said easily.

When Sebastian got back to the office he called his teammate back.

"What's up? Been watching the weather, you okay?"

"Yeah. But I need some information." Sebastian leaned back in his grandfather's chair.

"You came to the right place, always glad to be of service."

Wasn't that the truth? Gideon Smith was without equal as far as the men of Omega Sky were concerned when it came to anything to do with tech and information. Hell, the man had started playing video games when he was a toddler, and was making money hand over fist for his family selling gaming hacks in elementary school. When he was fourteen he dropped out of school and started working for a start-up gaming company in Silicon Valley. How in the hell he ended up a Navy SEAL was still a mystery to Sebastian. He figured only their lieutenant Kostya Barona actually knew Gideon's entire story, but right now that didn't matter. What mattered was that Gideon was a man who could help.

"So are you going to finally let me loose on that prick of a grandfather? It'd be fun to tank all of his political aspirations." Sebastian grinned as he looked around his grandfather's pretentious office filled with hundreds of pictures of him shaking hands with celebrities.

"Cool your jets. I need you to check out three names for me. Gianna Prentiss, she comes from a small town in Kentucky called Berea. She is really tight with a friend by the name of Jada Harlow. She sounded like she has a New York accent, I bet they have an NYU connection. Then there is someone named Etta Rose. Doubt that is her real name; she was running a high-end escort service out of New Orleans twenty years ago. I need all of this information as quickly as possible."

"Am I allowed to ask why?" Sebastian asked, curiosity in his voice.

"Gianna is staying here at my grandfather's place. I caught her breaking into my grandfather's desk looking for information on Etta Rose. She won't tell me why she wants the info, but I can tell it's personal. I know I didn't talk to you before I left on leave, but I got a letter from the old man that said he would give me answers if I came home." Sebastian's voice trailed off.

"Is this about your mom and dad?" Sebastian could hear the concern in his friend's voice. Gideon knew about his mother's murder and his dad's death.

"That's the only reason I would ever bother to breathe the old bastard's air again. The fact that Gianna's looking for something to do with Granddad that happened twenty years ago really has my senses tingling. But, for all I know, she could just be an opportunist who's just trying to swindle an old man."

"What does your gut tell you?"

"She isn't a swindler. All of this is connected," Sebastian said softly. He leaned forward and smoothed out the crinkled papers on the desk.

"All right, I'll have something for you by the end of the day."

"Thanks, I appreciate it."

After Gideon hung up, Sebastian looked at the old pages in front of him. They were handwritten letters, all on different letterheads. It took him an hour to read through all of them. They were all requests for Lazar to intervene on behalf of a prison reform bill that was coming up in nineteen ninety-six. They gave heartrending accounts on behalf of loved ones who had gotten ill or died in prison.

So far nothing in the drawer was getting him any closer to the answers he needed regarding his mother and father's deaths or the mysterious Etta Rose. He shoved everything back in and locked the desk back up. It was eight in the morning and he had no idea when his uncle would wake up, but he couldn't risk him finding him. There would still be tomorrow night to check things out.

Sebastian turned out the lights and went back to check on Gianna. When he got to the drawing-room, she was gone. There was no sign that she had ever been there. The kitchen was empty too. He went upstairs to make sure she was okay, but when he knocked on her door there was no answer. He tried the doorknob but it was locked. Apparently, she was well enough to get her ass in bed.

She should have packed her blow dryer. Instead, here she was trying to towel dry her hair with a baseball-sized bump on her head. No, this wasn't making her cranky at all. Gianna took another look at herself in the mirror and grimaced—she looked like death warmed over. She was normally pale, but right now her pale skin looked albino white, and she was sporting some really dark shadows under her eyes. Too bad she hadn't packed any make-up. Maybe she could just brush her dark hair forward and let it cover her face for the day.

She snorted, yeah, that so wouldn't work. Hell, even Jada had said there was no hope for her when they'd Skyped at noon. She still couldn't believe all the shit that Sebastian had been through as a kid. Then there was the stuff that Jada had been able to unearth about his military career. How in the hell she'd been able to pull up classified material was beyond Gianna, but she'd done it. Sebastian and his team were freaking scary. Thank God they were good guys.

Gianna opened the bathroom door just a smidge and when she saw that the hallway was clear, she made a run for her bedroom across the hall. She quickly dressed in what she considered her armor. Since she wouldn't have to leave the house, she didn't have to worry about comfortable shoes, so she was going to wear some of the clothes she'd packed to impress Lazar. Hopefully, they would work on his grandson and keep him off her back, and stop him from noticing her looking like the walking dead.

She shook out her green sweater dress with the scoop neck, the one that hit her just above her knees, and threw it on with her sheer gray tights. She paired that with the leather boots that slid up above her knee. They'd been a

New York purchase when she'd sold a couple of her designs to a store that wanted exclusive rights for a new bedding line they were starting. She'd made bank on that deal.

Gianna brushed and dried her hair for another ten minutes until she could feel it was shiny and dry, then she headed for the kitchen.

"You're not going to tell me what I can and cannot do," she heard Armand say belligerently.

"I wasn't. I was offering some advice."

Gianna pushed open the swinging door and found Sebastian seated at the small kitchen table drinking coffee with Armand standing over him with his fists clenched. He was wearing his coat and boots.

"If I want to drive the four miles into town, that's my prerogative, and your punk Army ass isn't going to stop me."

Gianna walked to the counter where the coffee maker sat and pulled out a mug. "Navy, Armand. He's in the Navy."

"Doesn't matter, he's a punk."

Gianna poured herself a cup of coffee and went to the fridge to get out the creamer. After she was done doctoring up her coffee, she sat down at the table.

"I'm hungry, I feel like French toast. Since I'm going to cook, can I make some for either of you?" she asked as she sipped the extremely good coffee.

"It's lunchtime." Armand glowered at her. "The storm has subsided, so I'm leaving."

Gianna cocked her head. The wind might not be howling the way it had last night, but it was still loud.

"Armand, the roads are going to be shit," Sebastian said. "What's so important in town that won't wait until tomorrow?"

"That's none of your goddamned business, boy." He pulled car keys out of his pocket, then hit the kitchen door so hard that it swung wildly as he left toward the front door of the house. Gianna could hear the heavy winds when the front door was opened, even from her seat at the kitchen table.

"I'm not thinking he's making a wise decision," Gianna said as she took another sip of coffee.

"I'm not thinking that 'wise' is part of his make-up," Sebastian said as he got up and opened up the refrigerator. Gianna watched as he pulled out a carton of eggs and milk.

"What are you doing?"

"Helping you make breakfast." He also pulled out half of a ham that had been wrapped up in plastic wrap. "What do you think of fried ham to go along with the French toast?" he asked.

"Sounds good to me," she said as she started to get up.

"Stay there, Gianna. I'll cook. How does your head feel?"

"Not bad. I took some pills that I had in my purse before coming down, plus the caffeine is helping."

He pulled out a frying pan from a cupboard beneath the stove, he seemed to know his way around the kitchen. "Well, that's good." He started slicing off pieces of ham. "How did you like attending NYU?"

Gianna set down her mug of coffee. "Well, that didn't take long." She got up and grabbed a whisk off the rack where the utensils were kept. "How much intel were you able to find out in just seven hours?"

She picked up the eggs and milk and moved over to another counter, then looked for the cinnamon on the spice rack.

"A fair amount. Seems like the textile business is pretty lucrative." He shot her a smile over his shoulder. "It's also nice all that you've been doing to help out your cousin with her craft store in Berea."

Gianna started to whisk the ingredients for the French toast. "And Etta Rose, did your source find out anything about her?"

"Gideon was able to find out about Etta Rose and Jada Harlow."

Gianna stopped stirring and whipped her head around to face Sebastian. "How did you know Jada's last name?"

"Honey, her full name popped up on your phone last night."

Her shoulders fell. "Well, okay then."

"You didn't tell me; how did you like NYU?"

"Cut the hooey, Sebastian. We're not on a date. I want to hear what you found out about Etta Rose."

Sebastian turned over the ham slices, then nodded at the loaf of bread next to the other pan on the stove. She went over to it and turned on the heat, then turned to him and crossed her arms over her chest. "So?"

"Gotta give a little before I'm willing to share," he said as he went back to the table for his cup of coffee. "I still don't know what Lazar has to do with you."

Gianna dipped two pieces of bread in the batter and put them into the skillet. "My mom was once an escort for Etta Rose, and Lazar was one of Etta Rose's biggest clients. I want to find out if he knew my mom." She waited to see how he would take that.

"I know a little bit about your background, Baby. From what I found out about Etta Rose, it doesn't sound like your mom was the type to be one of her girls," he said gently.

"Then you only got part of the story." Gianna flipped over the slices of toast and soaked another one in batter. "Shelby Fayette, my mom, got an academic scholarship to

Loyola, but she still needed to work to afford housing, and her parents were sending money from home. I found her old roommate and she talked to me last year." Gianna plated the first pieces of toast.

"What did the roommate say?" Sebastian asked.

"It took a lot for her to finally talk to me. I had to show her the police report that had been filed when they found me before she would say anything. She'd tried to talk Mom out of going to work for Etta Rose, but she knew her parents couldn't afford much. Not a lot was said around the campus, but the few girls who had worked or were working for Etta were doing well for themselves, and it had never leaked out, so mom went for it."

Sebastian set the table, grabbed orange juice while Gianna finished plating the French toast and ham. They sat down at the table.

"What else did you find out?" he asked after they started to eat.

"According to Mom's roommate, everything was fine. She was paying all of her bills and even had money in savings, but then she took a couple of long weekends to Baton Rouge. Mom had even suggested that she should go as well because there would be really good money to be made, but Lori wasn't having it. After the Baton Rouge trips, Mom started to act squirrely. Two months later she didn't come home after one of the weekends. Lori filed a missing persons report, but never said anything about Etta Rose. She didn't want any of the other girls at Loyola to get into trouble. My grandparents were beside themselves. They thought she was dead. Lori told me that a year after she disappeared she showed up on Lori's door, thirty pounds lighter, beat to shit, strung out, and begging for money. She brought her inside to get her something to eat, then when she went to the kitchen she came back and mom had stolen her purse and was gone."

Gianna's eyes were burning. She couldn't bring herself to eat a bite of food.

"Jesus, Gianna, I'm so sorry."

She nodded, not looking up. "So I take it you didn't find all of that out?" she murmured.

"Gideon found the police report and the C.P.S. report. I know that six years after Shelby's disappearance from Loyola she was found in a crack house with her pimp, Jerrold Prentiss, and you. I know that by the grace of God she told C.P.S. about her folks in Kentucky and they came and got you, and that they tried to take her home too, but by the time they went back to the crack house, neither Shelby nor Jerrold could be found."

Still staring down at her full plate, Gianna nodded.

Sebastian pulled her hand off her lap and brought it to the table so he could twine his fingers with hers. "You need to eat."

"I thought you wanted to know how I was connected to Lazar."

"You told me. He was a client of Etta Rose, and your mom worked for Etta. That's enough for now." He tipped his head down to her plate. "Eat."

7

"Goddamn fool."

Sebastian and Gianna watched as two men half dragged, half carried Armand up the front stairs of the main house.

"Gianna, get back inside, there's no point you getting all wet," Sebastian said as he looked over at her.

She shot him a dark look, then turned around and went back down the hallway.

As the three men got closer, Sebastian could see that there were a couple of bruises on Armand's face. Who in the hell had he pissed off?

"Bastian, is that you?"

He took a closer look at the red-headed giant of a man on the right and broke into a grin. "Callum?"

"Nah, I'm the other O'Malley, Fergus. You never could tell us apart." He pushed Armand onto the other man and sprinted up the stairs to enfold Sebastian into a bearhug. "Jesus, man, it's good to see you. Wait 'til I tell Ma you're in town, she'll be wanting to feed you and setting you up with one of the cousins in no time."

"The food I'm good with, but no more set-ups with O'Malley girls, they scare me."

"That's smart on your part." Fergus turned so that they could both look at Armand being helped up the stairs. "This here is Bill. He and I drew the short straws and had to bring your numb-nuts uncle home. This is the fifth time this year that he's started a fight at The Anchor. If he didn't pay double for clean-up, they wouldn't let him back in each time."

The three of them went into the house and were met by Gianna who was holding a stack of towels and a first-aid kit. "Bring him into the kitchen and I can help get him cleaned up."

Sebastian saw Bill's and Fergus' eyes light up as they gave Gianna the once-over. He couldn't blame them—all that sexy, wavy dark hair that flowed down over that form-fitting sweater dress, what wasn't there to like?

"Hi, Gee!" Armand slurred out the greeting. "Miss me?"

She rolled her eyes.

"Follow me."

"Bastian, I'm liking the company you brought," Fergus muttered under his breath as they all followed her into the kitchen. Sebastian wasn't going to tell the big Irishman any differently. With all that was going on, he really didn't need him sniffing around because of a pretty face.

"My name is Gianna, how many times do I need to tell you that, Armand?" Gianna asked as she pulled out one of the kitchen chairs for Bill to drop him into.

"You love it when I call you Gee, and you know it." He tried to make a grab for her, but she backed up before he could. He would have fallen on the floor if Bill hadn't caught him and shoved his ass back into the chair.

"Okay, I'm not playing Florence Nightingale to this idiot, you are." She shoved the first aid kit at Sebastian, then crossed her arms and glared at Fergus. "What in the hell happened? He was only gone for five hours."

Armand chuckled. "I'm just that good."

"Shut it," she growled.

"Big Red, answer me." She pointed at Fergus.

Fergus nudged Sebastian with his elbow. "Seriously, Bastian, I like her, she's feisty. How'd you two meet?"

Gianna gave Fergus a confused glance. "Oh, we're not together. I'm renting the carriage house out back. I just met Sebastian yesterday when he came home."

Sebastian watched as both Bill and Fergus gave him long looks, then turned to look at Gianna.

"Is that right?" Fergus asked. He kicked out the legs of one of the kitchen chairs and sat down. "So tell me about yourself, sweet thing, and don't leave anything out."

Gianna shook her head. "Flirt much?"

"Bastian, your uncle is bleeding on the floor, shouldn't you be taking care of that?" Fergus asked, not taking his eyes off Gianna.

Sebastian grabbed Fergus' arm and hauled him up.

"What? Whoa, when did you get strong?" Fergus asked as he stumbled across the kitchen.

Sebastian looked over at Bill. "Both of you need to leave now. Gianna and I will take care of Uncle Armand. Wanna thank you boys for taking such good care of him."

Fergus let out a loud laugh and slapped him on the back. "Bring Gianna to dinner on Sunday. Ma will love to meet her."

Sebastian narrowed his eyes as he continued to escort Bill and Fergus toward the front door. When the door was finally open, and Bill and Fergus were on the porch, Fergus turned to him. "Man, it's really good to have you back. Hope you intend to stay for more than a minute. Some of us have really missed you."

Sebastian felt some of the knots that had been forming in his stomach since he'd gotten on the plane to come to Louisiana begin to loosen. He'd forgotten some of the good things about home.

"Where's Armand?"

"I sent him up to his room without supper."

She watched as he scrubbed his fingers through his hair and gave her a frustrated look.

"Wanna tell me what in the heck was with the whole caveman attitude? I'm pretty sure I just met you yesterday."

"I think I just regressed to my high school days with Fergus; it was a knee-jerk reaction." He gave her a half-grin. Shoot, that grin sure was potent.

"So you guys were close? Is that why he mentioned his mother cooking you dinner?"

"Yeah."

She thought about all she had heard from Jada today, and what a messed up life he'd had, what with losing his mom and dad and then living in this godforsaken house with Lazar. She was glad there were some good times for him. He slowly sat back down at the table across from her.

"How about you? Besides Jada, were you close with many people?"

She looked at him and felt a shiver run through her. It felt nice that this good-looking man would be asking her such a question. It felt so personal, like he really wanted to get to know her.

"Berea is a really small town, and a lot of people are poor and wear hand-me-downs. But the bad part is, everybody knows everybody else's business. Even though I was being raised by my granny and Pawpa who was a deacon of the church, I was still considered trash because they knew my mom was a prostitute. Not a lot of parents would allow their children to associate with me, which is why I wanted to go to a big-city university."

Sebastian nodded. "I could see that."

"What about you?" she asked gently.

"You did your homework, right?" he asked.

"Yep, I know about your parents. They died within months of one another."

"My mom was killed. Murdered. They never found her killer. She had custody of me up until then. Dad had me every other weekend and I hated it. I'd have to come here. The only saving grace was Philly. I have no idea why he even bothered with that custody arrangement since it didn't seem like he wanted to spend any time with me." Sebastian shook his head, lost in memory.

"What was your mom like?"

"She died when I was eight. She was strict, but in a good way. Made me eat vegetables and do my homework. We lived in Thibodaux, and she worked the main desk at a car dealership there. They loved her. She was beautiful, funny, and smart. At the dealership, she was the first person people saw when they came in. I sometimes got to come in and stay in the breakroom when she worked late."

"She sounds wonderful." Gianna reached out and covered his fist with her hand. He turned his over and twined his fingers with hers.

"We lived in this two-bedroom apartment, and now that I think about it, it doesn't make sense. She should have been getting a hell of a lot more in child support. As an adult, there are a lot of things that don't make sense."

Gianna nodded. He was right; it didn't make any sense. But this wasn't anything that Jada had uncovered. Instead, she had pulled up the old police files on the unsolved murder. Pamela Durand's car had been found in the parking lot of the long-term care facility where her mother lived on the outskirts of Thibodaux on one of the weekends that Sebastian was with his father. It was after she'd visited her mom. It had been unlocked, with her purse and phone inside. Three days later her body was found in a culvert near Raceland. She'd been shot in the back of the head.

"Did you ever look into things as an adult?" she asked.

Sebastian shook his head, his jaw tight.

"But that's why you're here now, isn't it?"

He nodded. His fingers tightened their grip on her hand as he looked off at nothing.

"Nothing makes sense out of that year. Then there was living here in *his* house after Dad died. Thank God for Philly and Neil."

Gianna could picture that.

"I'm so sorry that you had to go through that," she whispered softly.

"I had Gideon pull the police report. The bullet wound was her only injury, so I can take solace in that, but her murder has never been solved."

Gianna knew that.

Sebastian looked back at her, his gaze fierce. "I remember months before my mother died, Dad and my grandfather arguing about her. Grandpère was pissed. Said something about how she was trouble. After she was killed I confronted Dad, and he said I was confused. A month later he was dead."

"What happened after that?" she asked.

"I acted out. I got in so many fights in school and I was suspended so often that I would have been kept back a grade if I weren't Lazar's grandkid."

"How long did that go on?" she asked.

"It wasn't until I took on the O'Malley brothers and they wiped the floor with me. Then they laughed it off and took me home with them. Of course, the O'Malleys weren't good enough for me to be friends with in Grand-père's eyes, so I'd only see them when congress was in session."

Gianna grinned. She liked the idea of him having friends like Fergus growing up.

"He's a flirt, you know."

"Yeah, I caught on to that." She pulled her hand away and started piling up the plates so she could take them to the sink. She needed to think.

Gianna wasn't surprised when Sebastian came up beside her and brought over the whisk and mixing bowl.

"You were pretty confident you would be invited to stay when you showed up with your little trailer, huh?" Sebastian gave her a look out of the corner of his eye.

"That was just my first ploy. If that didn't work, I figured I could knock on the front door and tell Lazar that I was writing a book about famous Louisiana statesmen, and he deserved at least three chapters."

Sebastian let out a long laugh. "Yep, that would have done it. Why didn't you lead with that?"

"Because then I would have been forced to pander to him all the time. This way I got to work on my sketches."

She rinsed her hands after putting the last dish in the dishwasher and turned to Sebastian. "It seems to me that you and I have a lot in common."

He raised his eyebrow. "Hmmm."

Darn, he's going to make me work for it.

"Yeah, it looks like we both want to know what happened to our mothers."

He nodded.

She shoved her hands on her hips. "For God's sake, Sebastian. Do I really need to spell it out!"

He crossed his arms over his wide chest and gave her a small grin. "Yep."

"I think we should work together."

He shook his head. "Sorry, *cher.* I work alone."

She saw red, but then her vision cleared. "That is total hogwash. SEALs work in teams. You are totally a team player."

"And you aren't one of my teammates."

"Two heads are better than one."

"*Cher,* I saw your sleuthing abilities last night. You almost knocked yourself out. I'm going to be better off on my own."

Gianna took a deep breath. Time for a new tactic. "All righty then, I won't tell you about the LLC out of Delaware that Jada dug up." She headed for the kitchen door. She wasn't surprised when he didn't follow her, but he would. She knew he would.

8

"Man, you've got to give me more than an LLC out of Delaware. There are hundreds of thousands of those," Gideon said.

"You're the information genius, don't tell me some NYU student can find something you can't," Sebastian baited his friend.

"I told you, Jada is a whole lot more than that."

Sebastian heard both frustration and admiration in his teammate's voice.

"Sorry, I don't mean to be an asshole. Not enough sleep."

"No worries. But I've got to tell you, I don't think it is a bad idea for you and Gianna to work together."

Sebastian pulled his phone away from his ear and looked at it to see if the name on the screen said Gideon Smith. It did. "I'm sorry, are you suggesting I work with the woman who paints sheets?"

Gideon laughed. "Point number one, anyone who can make that much money designing sheets is someone I admire. Point number two, I say hell yes. You two have matching agendas."

Sebastian leaned back in his grandfather's leather chair. Fuck, he'd been thinking the same damn thing.

"Gideon, my mom was basically executed. Gianna is five foot nothing. I don't want her near this situation."

"Point number one, that was twenty years ago. Point number two, do you want her going off on her own, or do you want to be working with her so you can watch out for her?"

"You know how annoying it is when you talk in bullet points, right?"

Gideon chuckled. "Yep."

"You know it's even more annoying when you're right, right?"

"Yep."

"Fuck." Sebastian dug his fingers deep into the tense muscles in the back of his neck. "What else you got for me?"

"I have a hunch about Etta Rose."

Sebastian sat upright. "Yeah?"

"I got to thinking—how would she know which girls to target at the universities? Then I remembered the age-old rule of 'follow the money.' Gianna's mother was getting tuition aid, so I tracked down who had access to that. There are six different women who fit the bill in the Louisiana area during that time who would know the financial situations of young co-eds. I'm running some cross-searches right now. The only problem is, our Etta Rose could have just been paying someone for the intel, so that widens our search again. Or I could be full of shit."

"There is that. I doubt it. But the full-of-shit option is always on the table."

Gideon chuckled again. "I'll get back to you tonight."

"I appreciate it."

Sebastian got up and went to the office door and opened it. Gianna was leaning against the opposite wall with her ankles crossed.

"How long were you planning on waiting there?"

"I was just waiting until you were done with your phone call."

"The door is thick; you couldn't hear my call from where you were standing," Sebastian said.

"I had my ear to the door for the conversation. Unfortunately, everything was muffled."

Sebastian looked up at the ceiling for guidance. "You might as well come in."

"So are we a team?"

"I haven't decided."

"How about if I told your uncle I was worried about him and convinced him to take a sleeping pill so he would sleep better tonight."

"Why in the hell would he need that? The bastard drinks half a bottle of brandy most nights."

"He wasn't drinking. He was on the phone with a friend of his and said he needed his head clear. He was actually drinking water."

"What?"

"I know, right? So can I come in?"

Sebastian waved her into the office and she sat down in one of the chairs in front of the desk. "So where did you get the sleeping pill?"

"I found a bottle in your grandfather's medicine cabinet."

"You've really been through his bedroom and bathroom?"

"Yep." She popped the 'p' at the end, and Sebastian grinned. "I also found his Viagra."

"Jesus, I didn't want to know about that."

"I wasn't too thrilled either. Anyway, it tells me he's probably still paying for sex."

Sebastian thought so too. "So who in the hell was Armand talking to?"

"I really wasn't sure, he wasn't making a whole heck of a lot of sense. It sounded like an old buddy of his from college. He was trying to calm him down."

"Armand was trying to calm someone else down. That must have been interesting."

"Tell me about it," Gianna agreed. "So what's the plan, partner?"

Sebastian's eyes narrowed. "The plan is that you will be the silent partner who does exactly what I tell them to do."

Gianna got up from her chair and started walking around the side of the desk. "Okay, sure. Did you get into the drawers?"

Sebastian looked up as she stood over him. Now she was wearing tight jeans and a long-sleeved patterned top that hugged her figure lovingly. "Gianna, you're not hearing me. My grandfather comes home tomorrow. From everything you've told me about Etta Rose, and the things that Gideon is gathering, this is serious. You're not going to get any more involved than you already are."

Instead of shoving her hands on her hips as he expected, she bit her lip and tilted her head. He tried to discern if she was trying to play him. "You're serious, aren't you?" she asked softly. He saw that her eyes had gone soft. He nodded.

"You can't protect everyone, you know that, don't you?" she asked softly.

Talk about a gut punch.

"I might not be able to, but I can protect you."

"Both of our mothers died. I don't know if your grandfather was directly involved, but I would bet my last dollar he was at least indirectly involved. I'm not going to stop until I find out what happened."

A picture of his mother's smiling face flashed before his eyes. She was as young as Gianna was now.

"I'll blow your cover," he threatened.

"No, you won't, Honey." Her voice was soft and intimate in the dim light of the office. "You won't because it will tip off your investigation."

His lips twisted and Gianna's eyes went even softer. She lifted her hand and cupped his cheek. "You need to trust me. I can take care of myself."

He grabbed her hand and clasped it tight to his face. There wasn't a chance in hell he was going to allow her to get any more entangled than she already was, but he wasn't going to fight her tonight. Tomorrow when Grandpère came home, he'd make sure she was protected.

Gianna knew she'd won the battle when Sebastian unlocked all of the file drawers and had her help him go through them. The desk files held nothing of interest, but finally, they hit pay dirt with the last drawer on the credenza.

"Holy guacamole, do you see this?" Gianna exclaimed.

Sebastian chuckled. "You've been pointing to the same invoices for two minutes, *cher.* Kind of hard for me to miss."

"They're invoices from Rosie Ettabaum! That has to be her. Catering, my butt."

"Calm down there. This does not solve all of our problems."

She liked that he was now sitting on the floor with her.

She'd always studied and sketched on the floor, and when she started to go through the files, Sebastian had sat down next to her. It felt good.

"What do you mean it doesn't solve all of our problems? Now we know who she is, and Jada can track her down." Gianna had already pulled out her phone and was dialing. When she got Jada's voicemail, she hung up and instead texted her to call back.

She looked up and saw Sebastian taking a picture of the invoice.

"What are you doing?"

"I'm sending this to my guy. This should help with the investigation he's doing."

"Should Jada and your guy be working together?" Gianna asked.

"We'll see," he murmured, as he divvied up the pile of papers and gave her half. "Let's get through these. I don't know about you, but I'd like to get a little bit of sleep before my grandfather gets here, and it's already six in the morning."

Gianna looked down at her phone, surprised to see that Sebastian was right. "Wasn't there flooding? Will your grandfather be able to make it here?"

"I don't know how much has changed, but he's been known to take a helicopter from the state capitol, so I would expect to see him here today. Haven't you noticed the helicopter pad?"

Gianna shook her head.

"Yeah, well. He likes his perks."

She looked at the man who was seated next to her. "Was there any time that you actually liked your grandfather?"

"No. My earliest memory of him was when he was yelling so loudly at my mother that spit was hitting her face. I thought he was going to slap her."

"Did he ever hit her?" Gianna asked.

"No."

Gianna swallowed, then asked. "Did he ever hit you?"

"It doesn't matter."

She reached out to stop him from leafing through the papers in his hands. "Yes, it does."

He set the papers on the floor and gave her a soft smile. "*Cher,* it was a long time ago, it really doesn't matter. I'm grown, and I'm fine. But the fact that an adult would abuse a child? That tells you a whole hell of a lot about the man. So do I think he could have something to do with both of our mothers' deaths? Yes. Yes, I do."

Gianna lowered her head and blinked fast, not wanting him to see how badly his words had affected her.

"Hey," he reached up and tipped her chin up. "It's okay. Like I said, it was a long time ago." He tucked a lock of her hair behind her ear. "And Gianna, when I read the police report about you I wanted to cry too. I couldn't imagine any parent not wanting to love and care for you."

Her chin wobbled. "Stop."

"I can't."

She watched in fascination as he bent his head and his lips met hers. It started out as a sweet and tender kiss, but as soon as her lips parted, heat raced through her veins. Her hands shot up and speared through his hair, needing to make sure he didn't leave her. Teeth and tongues clashed. Sebastian tilted her head to get a better angle and the kiss went even deeper. She heard his groan then she moaned as he pulled her up into his lap.

The stubble on his chin scraped along her cheek as he traced kisses down her jaw.

"No," she mewled. She pulled at his hair so that she could slam her lips against his. She bit at his lower lip, then thrust her tongue into his mouth, reveling in his taste.

"Wildcat." He breathed the word before taking over the kiss. Gianna moved one hand so that she could push up under his shirt, needing to feel the heat of his skin. As soon as she touched him, she sighed her pleasure into his mouth. He sucked her tongue into his mouth and she melted deeper into his arms.

She pushed her hand up and up, loving the satin smoothness of his back over the thick muscles. She took her time, stopping, kneading, and scratching.

"*Cher,* you're killing me." His hands began a trail of their own down her back until they squeezed her ass. Gianna squirmed as her core was drenched with heat. She'd never been so turned on in her life.

"Sebastian," she moaned, trying to push even closer. She began tugging at his shirt, attempting to pull it over his head. Her legs began to twist and she heard paper tearing. It took a moment to figure out what was going on.

"Oh no." She pushed at Sebastian's chest.

"What's wrong, *cher*?"

She scrambled back up into a sitting position and saw where the heels of her boots had ripped some of the papers on the floor. When Sebastian saw what had her upset, he pulled her back into his arms. "It's fine, Gianna."

"No. I ruined it."

He kissed the top of her head. "It's going to be fine," he whispered again. His warm hand stroked her long hair down the length of her back, and she felt herself melt into his embrace.

They stayed like that for a long time before Gianna pushed back and looked up at him. "I have a question."

"Okay," he smiled gently. "Shoot."

"How didn't Ophelia know you were being abused?"

Gianna watched as Sebastian's face morphed into rage. "He never hurt me in a way that would show over my clothes." Sebastian's words were quiet. "He told me that if word ever got out that I'd been beaten, he'd tell everyone it was Neil that had done it, and he'd end up in prison."

Gianna gasped.

"He would have, too. It all stopped when I was thirteen. I ripped that stick out of his hands and knocked him to the ground. He was cowering beneath me, but he told me if I hurt him, he'd say that Neil had done it." He stared down at Gianna. "I hate that his blood runs through my veins."

"Stop that," she whispered. "You've got to remember that you're also your mother's son. Trust me, I know. Think about my father."

Sebastian dipped his head so that his forehead could rest against hers. "You're right. Thank you, *cher.*"

9

Sebastian sat quietly sipping bourbon as his grandfather, and the other three men who had accompanied him in the helicopter, continued their conversation in the study. It took all of his training to stay calm and listen to the plans that his grandfather and his cronies had concocted.

"I pulled a few strings so his re-enlistment papers have been lost," one of the cronies, a bald man, said.

What the fuck?

Sebastian sat up straight.

How is that even possible?

Sebastian loosened his grip on his glass so that he didn't break it.

"And I had my girl register him in the primary, so that's been taken care of." Sebastian remembered the name of the bald man—MacDougal. He hadn't liked him from the start. He had a sweaty, limp handshake and kept kissing his grandfather's ass.

"What about you, Archie? Are we going to get any funding from the state level, or are we going to have to do this all on our own?" His grandfather pointed at the third man who was smoking a cigar and on his third glass of bourbon.

"Oh, I've got money coming out our ears. When I told people we have an actual Navy SEAL who will be running for State Legislature they were all sporting wood." Everybody laughed.

Sebastian struggled to remain in his seat and not storm out the door.

"Did you hear that, boy?" his grandfather turned to him. "You'll have this in the bag."

"I heard." Sebastian gave his grandfather a grim smile and wondered how fast he could get ahold of Kostya to find out what the fuck had happened with his re-enlistment papers. He sure as hell didn't want those held up, so his Lieutenant better get this shit straightened out as quick as fucking possible.

"I gotta tell you, Lazar, having two Durands in Louisiana politics makes me pretty goddamn happy," MacDougal said. "There are a lot of fucking things that need to get done, and you're the men to do it."

His grandfather shot him a dark look. "You know I always look at all sides of an issue, Fred, and my grandson will do business the same way."

Bullshit. I know how things operate; my grandfather is the greasiest pig in the pen.

"But Lazar—"

"Shut up, MacDougal," Fred barked. "Young Durand will do his job with honor, just like he has serving our country. Isn't that right, Bastian?"

Sebastian nodded. He just needed to last a little bit longer.

"Isn't Armand going to be pissed?" MacDougal asked.

"You leave him to me," Lazar said as he waved his arm. "Armand knows his place."

"That drunk couldn't get elected anyways," Archie pointed over at MacDougal as he took another sip of bourbon.

Sebastian snorted. *Dumb bastard can't even see the irony as he drains his third glass of bourbon in an hour.*

"We need to figure out who's going to run the campaign. Can't be Madelaine, cause she's running yours," Fred said as he glanced over at Lazar.

"I've got some people in mind," Archie chimed in.

"Don't forget, we're going to need Bastian to do a lot of photo ops, and some commercials. We'll need him wearing fatigues and holding a gun. That will be best, don't you think, boys?" Lazar asked the group.

Sebastian was done. He couldn't stand it another minute. He stood up. "It seems like you have this well in hand. I'm going to step out and take care of some business."

"What kind of business do you have to take care of?" Lazar shouted. "This is what's important."

"If I'm going to quit the teams, then there are a lot of things I need to do. There will be a lot of hand-offs required. I'll need to report in."

"Nonsense. Take your leave and never look back," Lazar glared at him. "Fred will cover your ass."

"Grandpère, we can't afford to have me leaving on bad terms, now can we? That would be bad for my political image."

Lazar leaned back in his chair and gave him a considering look. "You're right. Goddammit, you're absolutely right." He looked at the other men in the room with a broad smile. "He has a knack for this, boys. He's going to go far. He'll be sitting in D.C. before you know it."

Sebastian walked out of the office before he had to listen to his grandfather stroke his own dick anymore. He walked down the hallway to the kitchen to see if Neil and

Ophelia had arrived back from visiting their daughter and grandkids yet. If he could just get a hug from Philly, he knew he could cool down. When he pushed in the swinging door to the kitchen, he found Gianna sitting at the table instead.

Shit. As much as part of him wanted to see Gianna, and get a hug from *her*, the rest of him wanted to avoid her. He knew she would want to start trying to get involved in the past, and he wanted her safe.

"Hey, Sebastian," she smiled up at him. "I made coffee, want some?"

He took his mostly full glass of bourbon to the sink and poured it down the drain. Then he grabbed a mug from the cupboard and poured himself some coffee and sat down at the table with her.

"Big goings-on in the office, huh?" Gianna asked.

"You could say that." Sebastian concentrated on her beautiful face, allowing that to wash away some of his anger.

She stared at him. "Are you going to share?"

"This doesn't concern anything we were talking about the other night. I wish I could say that my grandfather has some kind of dementia, but instead, it's his normal delusions of grandeur."

"So no answers from your grandfather yet?"

Sebastian gritted his teeth. "Nope."

"Shoot. I'm so sorry, Sebastian. Do you think that after those men leave he'll sit down and give you some?"

He slammed his mug of coffee down so hard that hot liquid splashed on his hands. "I should have known he wouldn't provide anything."

Gianna winced. "But isn't that why you've been doing some of your own investigating?"

He rubbed the back of his neck, but it didn't help

loosen his tight muscles. "Yeah," he admitted. He shot up from his chair so fast, it tipped backward on the linoleum floor. "I'm just pissed I bought into his shit for even a nano-second."

Gianna rushed up to stand beside him. She rested her small hands against his chest. "No matter how bad our relatives are to us, we will always have a little part of us that will believe that they are redeemable."

Is she right? Or am I just an idiot?

Gianna's eyes flashed. It was like she was reading his mind. Then the little sprite reached up and grabbed fistfuls of his hair and pulled his head down as she went up on tiptoes and smashed her mouth against his.

Just how much bourbon did I drink?

Sebastian couldn't believe the sheer power of her kiss. Her tongue swept across his bottom lip, and he opened up and let her taste explode into his mouth. He reached down and cupped her ass, forcing her to wrap her legs around his waist. Gianna whimpered into his mouth as he strode across the kitchen and hoisted her up onto the counter.

One of Gianna's hands trailed down the front of his shirt, as she started kneading the muscles of his chest. Her whimpers heated his veins and sent the blood rushing to his cock. Sebastian tangled his fingers into her hair and pulled hard, forcing their lips to part. Gianna's eyes drifted open.

"Don't stop," she protested.

"I'm not." Her scooped-neck top had been driving him crazy, so he tugged it down and was rewarded with the sight of her beautiful breasts overflowing a red lace bra. "You're gorgeous," he whispered as he bent forward.

Shit!

He yanked up her top, then pulled her face into his chest just as the kitchen door opened.

"Well lookie here. Seems like Gee is willing to put out for a war hero."

Sebastian looked over his shoulder at his uncle. "Armand, turn right around and leave."

"I don't think I will," he said as he sauntered to the middle of the kitchen. "I want to know when you and our little renter have gotten so well acquainted."

Gianna shoved hard at Sebastian's chest. "Step back." Her voice was firm.

Sebastian looked down at her and saw her resolute expression. "Are you sure?" he whispered.

She rolled her eyes and shoved at him again. Sebastian took a step backward. She hopped off the counter, then wove past him so that she could confront Armand. "You know, Armand, if Sebastian decides to kiss me, that's his business."

"Looked to me like you were clinging to him like a spider monkey," Armand squinted at her.

She laughed. "How are those beer goggles working for you, Armand?" She twirled back to look at Sebastian. "Sebastian, it's like I told you, I'm only going to be in town for a little bit longer, so there really can't be anything between us. I hope you'll understand."

Sebastian unclenched his fists at Gianna's words. He'd been ready to beat the shit out of his uncle for disrespecting Gianna. Instead, he stood here in awe of how she was able to handle the situation.

Armand's head swung from Sebastian, then back to Gianna, then back again. He started to smile. "Shit, Bastian, guess the rumors are wrong; you SEAL types don't get all the pussy."

Gianna sucked in a shocked breath. "Armand, you should be ashamed of yourself using language like that!"

Armand lowered his head. "I'm sorry, Gee."

"I'm going back to the carriage house," she said with an outraged huff. "Don't expect to see me back here tonight."

Sebastian couldn't help but admire the way her jeans molded to her ass as she stormed out the back door. Then he quickly moved across the kitchen floor until he had his uncle by the front of his shirt. "Listen here, you old bastard. You stay away from her, do you hear me?"

"So she means something to you, huh?" Armand gave him a considering look.

Sebastian lifted him off his feet. "You better listen to me, you really don't want to make me angry."

He shoved him aside then slammed out of the kitchen. He needed to talk to either Kostya or Gideon.

Sebastian took the stairs two at a time as he hustled up to his room. God, he wanted to just take off and drive for a little bit, but that would set off the men in the library if they saw him leave. He checked the charge left on his phone, then tried to get ahold of Kostya. Thank God he picked up on the first ring.

"Sebastian. I think you need to come back to Virginia."

His body went on alert. "Are we gearing up for a mission?" he asked his lieutenant.

"I think that place is no good for you."

Sebastian's jaw clenched. Shit, Gideon must be worried about him and shared that with Kostya, because the only time that Kostya Barona's English was a little off was when he was really worried.

"It's fine. I'm fine. Look, I need you to check on something for me. I hear that my reenlistment papers might have been put on hold."

"What the fuck?" There was a loud thump. Kostya had

just hit something. "This is because of politics from New Orleans?" Kostya was incredulous.

"That's what some decrepit old man down here is saying. I need you to check up on this for me."

"I'm going to call Captain Hale right now."

Sebastian grinned when he realized that Kostya had hung up without saying goodbye.

Next up was Gideon Smith.

The call went to voicemail. He didn't leave a message, he texted instead, then he laid down on the bed and stared up at the ceiling, trying to get his temper under control. Being angry didn't solve anything. He'd learned that as a SEAL. Goddammit, he'd learned that!

He shut his eyes and kept picturing his mother. It was always the same memory that came to mind. She'd taken him to a waterpark and they'd laughed that entire day. She'd been so beautiful and happy and they didn't leave until the park had closed down.

His phone vibrated in his hand and he swiped over the screen to answer Gideon's call.

"I hear that the alligators will eat a body. If there's no body, they can't press charges. I'm thinking if me, Landon, and Ryker come down we can take care of some things for you."

Sebastian fought a grin.

"Are you telling me you think I can't handle feeding the gators on my own? I'm hurt."

"Just saying, man." He paused. "So what do you need?" Gideon asked.

"I told you what my prick of a grandfather said in his letter, right?"

"Yeah, that he had some answers regarding your mother's murder, and maybe even something on how your dad died."

Sebastian swung his feet over the side of the bed. "Yeah," he gritted out.

"I'm taking it that's not what happened?"

"Fuck no. Turns out he's arranged for my reenlistment papers to be lost, and he's already started a campaign for me to run for the state legislature."

He really needed to leave the house. Go for a run or something. If not, he was going to break something.

"Sebastian, did you hear me?" Gideon asked.

"What?"

"Man, it was like I told you before, the police records were shit on your mother's murder. They shit-canned that case. I was really hoping you were actually going to hear something from the old man, but since you aren't, I have the name of a local private agency that might be able to help. They're over in Mississippi."

"Grandpère knows something," Sebastian growled. "There's not a doubt in my mind."

"I'm still looking into that Etta Rose lead you gave me. Sex and shady deals go hand in hand."

"You thinking blackmail?" Sebastian asked.

"Could be. I'll see what shakes loose."

"I appreciate it. I'm going to take off for a while. I'll be in touch."

He hung up and headed down the stairs to his SUV. Who gave a fuck what Grandpère and his cronies thought? He needed some room to think.

10

GIDEON SMITH – NAVAL AMPHIBIOUS BASE, LITTLE CREEK, VIRGINIA

Gideon looked down at his phone, then tapped it against his chin. This was not fucking good. Sebastian was too close to the edge. He knew the backgrounds of almost every one of the members of the Omega Sky team. No, that was in his job description to know their backgrounds, but hey, information had always been his stock and trade. He'd always worried that one day Sebastian's past might come back and bite him in the ass, and today was the day.

Sebastian Lazar Durand the Second had been in politics since the eighties, and if there was a dirty deal in Louisiana state politics, his hand was in that pie. At least if there was money to be made. Gideon had been looking into all of the corrupt activity going on with Lazar to see if there would be some kind of motivation behind Pamela Durand's death —or Lazar's son for that matter. But then when Sebastian had him check into Gianna, Jada, and Etta Rose he'd been hit with a curve ball.

This Jada woman, she was something else. She'd really hit a goldmine with the parties that Lazar had hosted with Etta Rose's escorts. That was definitely a new lead.

Gideon looked at the time on his computer. Only five more hours until he needed to get his ass to the airport. There wasn't a chance in hell he was going to let his boy handle all of this on his own.

Gianna had tramped over to the side of the big house after sundown and saw that Sebastian's SUV was gone. Then at six the next morning she'd done another check she'd seen the same thing.

I've got it bad.

She looked down at her muddy boots as she toed them off on the porch before going back into the carriage house. Gianna looked around the little living room and yawned. She had it *really* bad, because she wasn't a morning person, but she'd woken up at God-awful o'clock thinking about Sebastian and had left the house. She pulled off her hoodie, went to her bedroom, and crawled back into bed, still thinking about Sebastian. Yep, she had it bad.

She woke up at the persistent knocking on the door. She was still in her pajama bottoms and tank top, so she put on her hoodie again and pulled back the drapes to see who was on the porch. She squealed with delight when she saw Ophelia.

"Yay! You're back," she cried as she swung open the door.

Ophelia stayed out on the porch and smiled. "You're looking good, Gianna."

"Come in. Come in." Gianna stepped back and waved the woman inside. Ophelia was wearing her normal outfit of black polyester pants and a brightly colored top. This time Gianna spotted a chunky, blue-beaded necklace.

"Honey, that necklace is gorgeous. Come sit down and

tell me about your trip, and tell me where you got that necklace; it matches your eyes perfectly."

Ophelia blushed. "My daughter made it. She's making jewelry now. Isn't it cute?" Ophelia held it away from her neck so that Gianna could admire it.

"These aren't just normal beads, what is that?" Gianna asked.

"Some of it is sea glass and this here is recycled rubber."

"This is amazing. It's exactly the type of thing I would love to sell at Tina's Treasures back home."

"Really?"

"Absolutely," Gianna insisted. "Can I make you some coffee?"

"No, Neil and I got home last night, then came here first thing this morning. I just wanted to check on you. Are you coming up for breakfast?"

"So, are the three men that Lazar invited still there?"

"Yep."

"Then, I think I'll pass. I'll just make something here. How about Sebastian, did he come home?"

Ophelia's eyes lit up like a Christmas tree. "I can't wait to see that boy. When Neil and I got here, there was no sign of him and he would have been the first one up. Armand and Lazar didn't know where he was, and Lazar is not happy about it. Apparently, he was out all night. So what do you think of my baby?" Ophelia asked Gianna.

Gianna snorted. "Baby?"

"Well, he was when he left. Are you trying to tell me he isn't a baby anymore?"

"I'll let you decide for yourself," Gianna demurred.

Ophelia pushed up off the sofa. "I better get back up there and start breakfast. By the looks of Lazar's office, they're probably hung over with how low the bourbon bottles are, but you never know."

Gianna got up and hugged the woman. "Thanks for coming to check on me."

"So, will I see you for meals if Sebastian is back?" Ophelia's eyes twinkled.

"I gotta tell you, even Sebastian won't be a big enough draw to outweigh Lazar's creepy cronies."

Ophelia threw back her head and laughed. "I really do like you, Gianna Prentiss."

Sebastian pulled in to the side of the house and saw an old Chevy pickup. His breath hitched. *Please God, say that Philly and Neil are back, because that's the only saving grace to this clusterfuck.*

He got out of his vehicle and opened the front door. It was past noon, so he was praying that the men were back at it in Lazar's office. As soon as he stepped over the threshold he looked down the long hallway and saw Philly standing there. She put her finger to her lips and beckoned him toward the back of the house.

He made it to the kitchen almost before she did. When he bent down to give her a hug, she pushed against his chest and shook her head.

"No. Absolutely not. Let me look at you, sweet boy."

His heart twisted when he saw the tears on her cheeks.

"Don't cry," he begged.

"And don't you be telling me what to do or not to do." She backed up another step and Sebastian did his best not to shift from foot to foot underneath her intense scrutiny. After a minute, her hands covered her mouth, and more tears fell.

"Philly, don't cry. Please don't cry," he begged. "I'm sorry I didn't call."

She shook her head wildly. "That's not it. Oh, honey, you've been hurt. You've taken on more scars."

Sebastian had had enough. He swept her back into his arms. "Now stop. You need to stop, Philly." He pressed her face to his chest. "Life's really good now. I'm exactly where I'm meant to be. I'm serving my country. I'm working with the best men in the world."

She continued to shudder, but then magic happened, as her arms crept around his waist and he was once again enveloped in a Philly hug.

"Oh, Sebastian. I've prayed for you every single day. Every single day, my sweet boy."

He closed his eyes and wasn't surprised when he felt wet on his cheeks.

"Then your prayers were answered, Philly. I'm healthy, whole, and happy."

He heard her snort. Then she pressed against his chest so she could tilt her head up and look him in the eye. "So you've got a girl? When are you going to give me grandbabies?"

Sebastian shouted with laughter.

"I love you, Philly. I love you so damn much."

That evening, Sebastian looked around the dining room table from his end of the table. He'd always hated this room. Lazar had insisted they eat in here and that Philly serve them, even when he had been eight years old, and it had just been the two of them. He looked around at all of the old men and grimaced. He was in hell. Philly was serving them again. Now that he was back, he needed to arrange for Philly and Neil to get new jobs.

"I expect you were out tying up those loose ends you

told us about," Lazar said from the head of the table. "Is that right, Bastian?"

"Something like that." Sebastian inclined his head. He ignored the wine and drank from his water glass.

Lazar's eyes narrowed.

"Armand, where is our lovely guest? I haven't seen Miss Prentiss since I've been back. You haven't run her off, have you?"

"I'm not the one you should be worried about running her off, Daddy. I think you should be looking at your golden boy." Armand waved his hand toward Sebastian. Armand had his glass in his hand, and some wine spilled out and hit Archie's sleeve.

"Goddammit boy, just how drunk are you?" Lazar yelled.

"I'm not drunk, Daddy, just feeling a little happy is all."

"Ophelia! Get in here," Lazar yelled to the second swinging door that led to the kitchen. "Ophelia!"

Sebastian stood up from his chair and banged his fists on the table, causing the dishes to jump. "Old man, do not *ever* yell at Ophelia like that again. Do you hear me?"

Lazar stood up and threw his napkin down on his plate. "Do not disrespect me in my own home, boy."

"Then learn some manners. We have guests. Don't holler at a woman who has been like a family member in this household for over twenty-five years."

Ophelia came out of the swinging door and placed the rib roast in the middle of the table. Then she stood there with her hands on her hips. She stared at Lazar.

Lazar looked from Ophelia back at Sebastian, then he sighed. "Bastian, you're right. These are stressful times. I don't know what I was thinking. Forgive me, son."

"I'm not the one you owe an apology to," Sebastian gritted out.

Lazar barely turned his head toward Ophelia. "My apologies."

Ophelia nodded, then left the room.

Sebastian waited for his grandfather to sit back down, then he did the same thing. He fucking hated this place.

Archie reached over for the rib roast. "This looks wonderful." He served himself a piece then passed it down to MacDougal.

"Well that went well," Armand said jovially. "Daddy, I have a bit of business up North. Now that the water's gone down and the bridge is passable, I'm leaving in the morning."

Lazar frowned at his son. "What in the hell are you talking about? I need you here working with Neil."

"Daddy, this is important."

Sebastian looked up from the meat he was putting on his plate, surprised at the almost adult-sounding tone coming out of his uncle's mouth.

"I don't give a shit, you're not leaving."

Armand put down his wine glass and took a sip of water, then started cutting into the rib roast.

11

Gianna held the sweater tight around her as she looked out the window to see who was knocking at her door. Her gut clenched when she saw it was Sebastian. She'd hoped—oh how she'd hoped—that it would be him at her door. He knocked again.

"Answer the door, Gianna. I can see your shadow in the window."

She trembled, then unlocked the door and opened it. He stood there. "Are you going to invite me in?"

She took a step backward. "Come in."

When she couldn't stand him staring at her another instant, she whirled away and stalked to the small kitchen. "Can I get you something to drink?" she asked as she stood in front of her open refrigerator.

Strong hands ran up and down her arms. "I'm not thirsty."

"Why are you here, Sebastian?"

She felt him rest his forehead on top of her head. "Is it bad that somehow when my world is out of control, and

I'm angry at everybody, I know I can come here and you'll make it all right?"

She thought about that night in the library. The night that she had been replaying over and over again. Sebastian the man. Sebastian the child. How had he burrowed so deeply into her heart? It made no sense.

"Gianna, did you hear me?"

She let him turn her around so that his arms held her. His fingers pushed up her chin so that their eyes met. "You barely know me." Even she could hardly hear the words she spoke.

"I know you," he breathed into her ear. "All the hurt that you've gone through in your life? All of your strength? I am in awe of you, and you bring me comfort."

She jerked away from him and leaned against the kitchen counter, putting space between them. "Sebastian if you came here just to have sex, then say it. You don't need to say the pretty words."

"Goddammit, Gianna, don't you think I know this sounds crazy? I'm not here for sex." He strode past her and into the living room, his hand raking through his hair until he ended up pulling the ends with his fist. He turned and glared at her. "I need to talk to one sane person in this world. One person who understands what it's like to have stink and rot swirling around them and wonder how to escape it."

How was that her? She'd never been anybody. The only thing close to anything that she'd done was her fabrics; that was her strength.

"I don't—"

He was on her in an instant, his hand covering her mouth. "I know what you're going to say, and I'm not going to stand for it. You're going to say some drivel about how you don't have anything to offer, right?"

How can he know?

He lowered his head, his lips at her ear. "That was what you were going to say, right?"

He lifted his palm from her lips. "I don't know. Maybe," she said.

"Calm. You gave me calm when all I've felt was rage since I came here. So how can you not be special?"

"What do you want from me, Sebastian? Just tell me what you want. Don't make me try to guess. I'll get it wrong, and then... and then..."

"Then what, *cher*?"

"Then you'll laugh." And wasn't that one of the worst ways she could be hurt?

"I would never laugh at you. Please trust me. Can you?"

She looked up into the dark depth of his eyes. She saw such anguish, but it was the hope that called to her.

"I'll try to trust you. But it's hard."

He pushed the cardigan off her shoulders. She let her arms drop so that it fell to the floor. Her breathing sped up as he looked at her thin tank top and lacy sleep shorts. She bit her lip and forced herself to stay still, even though every instinct was telling her to run and hide.

Sebastian reached up and cupped her cheek. His thumb brushed her lower lip, tugging it away from her teeth. "I'm the only one allowed to bite this lip."

His thumb continued to graze back and forth along her lower lip. It tingled, then it throbbed and then...then it burned. Gianna shuddered as Sebastian wrapped his other arm around her waist, helping her to stand.

"I want another kiss now," he said. His voice was so much deeper, it made her bones vibrate. "Can I kiss you?"

She nodded. She didn't have any words.

His mouth dipped down and devoured hers. His tongue pushed its way into her mouth, and she loved it. It was a maelstrom of flavors, heat, wet, and emotion. His tongue caressed hers, teaching her how to play, suck, and tease. The burning excitement rushed higher, and Gianna gripped his shoulders, knowing that if she didn't hold on, she would be lost.

She whimpered when he cupped her breast and brushed his thumb over her nipple. When he pushed up her tank top and rolled her nipple between his fingers, she let out a long moan of pleasure and she felt his smile against her lips. His head lifted and he looked down at her. He pinched her nipple harder and she started to pant. He peeled her tank over her head.

"You like that." He didn't bother asking a question.

"What else do you like, *cher*?"

She didn't know.

"Gianna, answer the question; what else do you like?" He tugged at her nipple, then bent down and took it into his mouth and sucked hard.

"Yes! More. I like that!"

When she felt his teeth, she hit his shoulder. He immediately stopped and looked down at her. "Did I hurt you?"

"No. Yes. I don't know," she wailed. "Just keep doing it."

Sebastian chuckled and took her other nipple into his talented mouth. Gianna's head fell back as if her head were a flower with a broken stem.

He kissed his way upwards and took her mouth again. Everything felt so good. Nothing had ever felt this good. She opened her eyes and studied his face. How was this possible? What was she supposed to be doing? Wasn't she supposed to be giving back? Sebastian's eyes slowly opened.

"Oh, *cher*."

"What?"

"We need to take this into the bedroom."

She shrieked when he picked her up. "Sebastian, you can't do that, I'm too heavy."

He threw back his head and laughed. She hit his shoulder and he was still laughing when he laid her down onto the bed. "My rucksacks are heavier than you are and I have to carry them for twenty miles." He kissed the tip of her nose. "But enough about that. You had your eyes open when we were kissing."

"So?"

"What were you thinking?"

"I'm not doing anything back. I should be doing for you."

He knelt back on his haunches. "Is that how things work in your world? Nobody does anything for you unless you've done something for them?"

She frowned. "Isn't that always the way?"

Sebastian sighed. "I guess it is."

Why did Gianna's words hit me so wrong? Wasn't she basically quoting back my belief system?

"Now what are you thinking so hard about?" she teased.

"Your breasts," he grinned. His palms covered her generous curves, loving the silky warmth. She wiggled beneath him and he knew he wasn't giving her what she needed. He squeezed and she began to relax. When he squeezed harder, she relaxed more. He brushed his thumbs over her nipples and her back arched. She was fucking gorgeous.

Sebastian was mesmerized by the tawny color of her nipples. Everything about her body made his cock ache. Hell, it wasn't just her body, it was everything Gianna that made him hard. He bent and sucked one nipple deep into his mouth while he twirled the other between his thumb and finger. He kept it up until her soft sighs became deep moans and she gripped his hair and begged him for more.

"What kind of more?" he asked.

Her face was flushed, her eyes were glassy. "I don't know. Just *more*."

Sebastian went to the waist of her sleep shorts and she stopped him. "No."

"What's wrong?"

"I can't be naked while you have all of your clothes on."

"That can be easily fixed." Sebastian climbed off the bed and pulled his long-sleeved shirt over his head. Gianna made a sound and he looked down at her. She was smiling. He smiled back. It was good to know that she liked how he looked.

This time when he started to unbutton and unzip his jeans, he watched her. When she licked her lips, his cock pulsed. Jesus, she was some sort of sex goddess and she had no fucking clue. Sebastian grabbed his wallet out of his jeans, then took out the condom and put it right beside the pillow. Then he pulled off his pants and was left in his boxer briefs.

"Is this enough? Can I take off your shorts now?" he asked.

She nodded.

"Thank fuck."

Sebastian curled his fingers beneath the elastic waistband and tugged, then he groaned when he realized she wasn't wearing panties. "Jesus, God."

Her eyes flew up to stare at him. "It's all good," he promised her. He softened his voice. "You're beautiful. I can't believe I'm here with you."

He watched as the anxiety fled from her face. He finished stripping the shorts from her legs, then tossed them on the floor. He ran his fingers from her ankles to the insides of her thighs until they touched the lips of her sex. Gianna trembled beneath him. Sebastian smoothed his palms outwards to stroke her curvy thighs, and then he cupped the back of her knees and coaxed them up and out. She whimpered. When he looked up, she had the crook of her arm over her eyes.

"No *cher*, no. This is good. You're beautiful."

She shook her head, her wild curls flying across the pillows in a glorious tangle. Everything about her was so lushly feminine he would be lucky to not come after his first stroke inside her. He looked down at her glistening sex and used his thumbs to part her lips so he could taste her. Her exotic flavor took over all of his senses, so much so that he thought he was drowning. Vaguely he could hear all of the little sounds she was making, and that only encouraged him to ensure he brought her the most pleasure possible.

Sebastian pushed two fingers inside of her, stretching her snug flesh, turning and probing until he found that spot that had Gianna crying out with pleasure. He brushed, stroked, and caressed her until she arched up the bed screaming his name, her rapture soaking his fingers. Now she was ready. He pulled off his boxers.

"God, yes." Gianna reached out and circled his straining flesh with her small hand, pumping his cock. "I need. Give me what I need," she moaned.

He opened the condom and rolled it on.

He slid his cock along her folds, caressing her clit with the tip of his penis. "That's good, but not what I want."

He grinned. "What do you want?"

She touched him again, pulling him toward her entrance. Arching up so that their bodies could merge. "This. This is what I want."

Sebastian pushed slowly inwards, watching Gianna's face, making sure there was no sign of discomfort. She glared at him. "I'm fine!" She wrapped her legs around his hips and thrust upwards...hard. There was no mistaking her cry of satisfaction.

Sebastian pushed the hair away from her face so that he could kiss her again. "I have never felt anything so good in my life."

"You know what would be better?" she asked with a grin.

"What?" he asked as he kissed his way down her jaw.

"If you darn well started moving!"

He threw back his head and laughed.

"Darn it, don't laugh. Move!"

Sebastian stopped smiling. His face turned serious and sensual. He began to slowly drive her out of her mind with thrust after thrust and stroke after stroke of pulsing heat. Gianna's head thrashed side to side on the pillows, her nails digging into Sebastian's back. "I can't stand it anymore. Stop."

"You're not there yet," he teased softly.

"But it feels so *good*," she groaned.

He thrust deeper and she started to pant.

"It's going to feel even better." He twisted, making sure that he hit that spot inside that he'd caressed with his fingers.

"Sebastian," Gianna wailed.

Stroke after stroke, he caressed her G-spot. He watched her grit her teeth and clench her jaw. He reached up and brushed his thumb across her bottom lip, then nipped her earlobe. "Come, Gianna."

She screamed.

12

Sebastian was pissed that he'd been sucked back into his grandfather's office so that Philly and Neil had already left for the evening before he'd had a chance to talk to her. So here he was, walking down to the carriage house. So he started down the barely used path that would take him down to the old pond.

His phone vibrated in his back pocket when the pond was in sight. It was Gideon.

"Hey. Any more info for me? I need something to sink my teeth into."

"Yeah, well, I do have some more intel," Gideon said. "I should be in front of your Granddaddy's house in ten minutes, because staying at the Gator Inn was a hard no. We need to get our asses up to Dallas to follow up on a new lead."

"Fuck, I can't believe you flew out here. Did you buy an apron and start baking cookies? Because you sure are acting like a mom, what with you coming down here to hold my hand and all."

"And seeing how you're choosing to flip me shit about

it, I see you're not mad. Instead, you're doing the smart thing and you're going to let me help." Sebastian could hear the relief in his friend's voice.

"I think you're an overprotective dumbass who is blowing his leave on stupid shit, but far be it for me to have an opinion." Sebastian was already jogging past the Carriage House. He needed to get back to his room and pack his duffel.

"Now you have as long as it takes for me to get there from the Gator Inn." Gideon chuckled, and the line went dead. Sebastian shoved his phone in his back pocket and bounded up the stairs to the kitchen door. Nobody saw him as he made his way upstairs. He had his duffel packed and the front door to the house opened when he heard someone shout his name.

"Where in the hell do you think you're going now?" Lazar came barreling down the hallway.

Sebastian shut the door and turned to look at Lazar. This time he really looked at him. He hadn't aged well at all. For a man who was seventy-four, he looked at least a decade older. He might have a good set of lungs on him, but he moved slowly. Sebastian was around a lot of former military men. They kept in shape; the same couldn't be said for his Grandpère.

"What are you staring at?" Lazar demanded to know when he was a foot away from Sebastian.

"You've been avoiding being alone with me. I want to know about the answers you promised me."

"And we'll get to that," Lazar sputtered. "But we have to jump on your campaign, son. This can't wait. The past is past. That's old news. We have plenty of time to hash over that," Lazar said as he rested his hand on Sebastian's shoulder.

Sebastian shrugged it off.

"What do you know about my mother's death? What happened to my father?"

Lazar's eyes widened and he reeled backward. "That was a terrible year."

Sebastian's fists clenched. "No need to tell me, I lived it. You said my mom was nothing but trouble and then she was murdered."

"I never said any such thing," he blustered. He looked over his shoulder to where his office was, then gripped Sebastian's arm. "Follow me."

Sebastian followed his grandfather into the empty kitchen. "They closed your mother's case. They figured it was something to do with drugs."

"Are you out of your mind, old man?" Sebastian roared. "I've read the case file. They didn't have shit, and nowhere in there did they say anything about it having to do with drugs. Hell, her purse and phone were left in the car. They worked the case for one damned week. One. Then they closed it because you didn't want them to find out what really happened."

Sebastian saw a flicker of fear pass over his grandfather's face before he turned red and pushed his finger into Sebastian's chest. "You have no idea what you're talking about. Of course, I had that thing buried. It was all over the papers, it needed to be shut down, your dad didn't need that kind of trash weighing him down."

Sebastian grabbed his grandfather's wrist and twisted, not caring about his cry of pain. "And that's what you always called her. Trash. So her murder was just one more thing about her that you just wanted buried. Or was it even worse? Did you have something to do with her murder?" Sebastian felt like he was encased in ice, his voice a low hiss.

"Bastian, how could you even ask me something like that?" he trembled. "She was your mother."

"Don't you dare lie to me, old man, you wanted her gone. How many times did I hear you say to Dad that marrying her was the worst mistake he'd ever made?"

Lazar didn't even try to wiggle out of Sebastian's grip. His eyes stayed glued to his grandson's. "I would never. Not *ever,* harm the mother of my grandson," he choked out.

Sebastian shoved him away. "You lying old fool. My mom scrimped and saved to give me a good life, while the good old Durands lived the high life. You harmed her all right."

Lazar threw back his shoulders. "I offered her good money to give your father full custody, all she ever had to do was hand you over and leave the state. It was her choice to live the way she did."

The words hit him like a ton of bricks. "Did my dad know about that?"

"He knew that I didn't want you to be living with that woman. You belonged here."

"That's not what I asked. Did he know that you'd offered to buy me?"

Lazar gave Sebastian a disgusted look. "Buy is an ugly word. I was trying to do what was best for you. And for her, for that matter."

Sebastian shook his head, trying to clear it. "And Dad? Did he know?"

Lazar shrugged. "Your dad knew that I was always trying to do the right thing for our family. He trusted me to do right."

Sebastian turned to leave, then stopped as his hand started to push the kitchen door. He turned back to Lazar. "And what about Dad's death? You don't actually believe he lost control of his car, do you?" He watched his grandfather intently.

"That was a long time ago," Lazar breathed out the words. "The day he died, I lost a piece of my heart."

Sebastian lifted his eyes to the ceiling, then looked back at his grandfather. "Cut the melodrama. Do you think he was killed too?"

Lazar stomped over to where Sebastian stood. "If there had been anything I could have found out, whether I could prove it in a court of law, that told me my son was murdered, I would have burned down this parish to make them pay."

Sebastian nodded. He left the kitchen, picked up his duffel by the front door, and went outside. There was a big, black Ford Two-Fifty idling in the front drive. He didn't even have it in him to smile when he saw Gideon; he just tossed his duffel into the backseat, then let himself into the passenger side and buckled in.

"Sebastian?" Gideon asked.

"Just drive."

At least this time she hadn't gotten up early; she'd made her junk food run last night, so she'd had enough to last her for days.

"So you're pissed," Jada said.

"I'm super, duper, angrily, grumpy," Gianna huffed as she dipped her fourth beignet into raspberry sauce and stuffed half of it into her mouth as she stared at her computer screen.

"Well, that sounds really grown-up. What are you eating?"

"Bwn-wwyay," Gianna answered.

"Gross! Don't talk with your mouth full. Now tell me what really has you so fucking mad. Three days you were practically farting rainbows, so what's wrong? I just e-mailed you more information on Rosie Ettabaum, so you should be all kinds of happy, not trying to eat your body weight in baked goods."

Gianna picked up another one of Louisiana's famous fried pieces of dough with powdered sugar. When she'd purchased them last night at Jimmy's Po-Boy, Jimmy had known enough not to make a crack when she'd bought two dozen of the doughy bits of goodness with raspberry sauce and then asked where she could buy some Hershey's chocolate syrup.

"I'm not mad. I'm happy. We have a lead." She dipped her beignet into the cup of warmed chocolate sauce and took a big bite.

"I'm not buying this sunshine. The last time you were this upset was when you found out the guy you had been dreaming about for over a year in your knitwear design class was gay. Which I had been telling you from day one, I might add," Jada smirked.

Gianna glared at the computer screen. It had been three days since Armand had caught Sebastian and her kissing in the kitchen, and since then she'd only seen Sebastian once in passing and he'd barely said one word to her. When she'd tried to get him off to the side to talk to him, he had side-stepped her. How were they going to work on the case if he wouldn't talk to her? What's more, how were they going to kiss again if they didn't get an opportunity to be alone together?

"Gianna, talk to me. Tell me what's wrong before you buy out the kid's cereal aisle at the Piggly Wiggly. The last time you did that you didn't come down off of the sugar high for thirty-six hours."

Gianna glared at her computer. "It wasn't that bad."

"It so was. You ate a box of Fruity Pebbles, Fruit Loops, Trix, and two boxes of Apple Jacks. It's amazing you didn't go into a diabetic coma."

"It was somewhat healthy. They all had fruit in them," she mumbled.

"Tell me what's wrong," Jada demanded.

"Sebastian kissed me. Twice. They were the best kisses ever."

"Girl!"

"But that's not all. We, um..." Her voice trailed off.

"*Girl*!" This time, Jada's voice was practically a growl. "You did the nasty?"

"And *that* was the best nasty ever." She sighed. "But now he's disappeared. There. Are you happy now?"

Gianna pushed back her computer from her lap and shoved the plate of food to the foot of the bed. She shot off the bed and headed to her closet.

"Hey, where are you going?" Jada shouted.

Gianna grabbed her smallest suitcase out of the closet and tossed it onto the duvet, then bent down so she could look at the computer screen.

"I'm out of here."

"You're leaving Louisiana? Are you going home?"

Gianna marched over to the bed and bent sideways to look into the computer screen. "Are you bananas? Of course I'm not leaving Louisiana."

"Are you moving out of the Durand house?"

"No," she said sarcastically. "I'm taking a little trip."

"Why? I thought you said you were getting sketches done, and dealing with your suppliers."

"I was. I mean, I am." Gianna unzipped the suitcase then stormed over to her dresser and grabbed some underwear. "I was also waiting here like a dumbass thinking Sebastian was going to come over and we would work together like a team while I waited for you to get back from that conference you had to attend in Miami. I tried to run some searches on Rosie Ettabaum, but I didn't get very far."

Gianna went to the closet and grabbed two dresses and rolled them up.

"Calm down, girl. You did great. The legwork you did gave me a head start, for real."

Gianna picked up her laptop so that she could stare directly into her friend's face. "You are full of baby poop."

"*Shit,* Gianna," Jada growled. "I'm full of shit. So what if I am?" Jada twisted her neck back and forth, in a way that told Gianna she was getting angry. "Computer research is just not your thing."

"Well, I'll tell you what is—being sneaky. So I'm going to follow up on the name I got off Armand's phone. I'm sick of staying here."

"Hey, wait a good goddamn minute!" Jada screeched when Gianna put down the computer and went into the bathroom to gather up her cosmetics. She ignored all of Jada's caterwauling as she put everything she would need into her make-up bag. When she came back out into the bedroom, Jada was still talking.

"Answer me!"

"I told you I had other leads," Gianna said belligerently.

"Cut the shit, girlfriend. Just because you're not getting laid by SEAL boy, doesn't mean you need to get all snarky with me. Now sit your happy ass down and tell me what name you got off of Armand's phone before I come down to Louisiana and whip your damn ass."

Gianna sat down on the bed and started zipping up the suitcase. "I told you that when I gave him the sleeping pill I went back and checked his phone history. That call he'd been on was all sorts of weird."

"So give me the name and I'll trace it for you," Jada coaxed.

Gianna smiled at her friend. "You just keep on that lead for Etta Rose or Rosie Ettabaum and I'll check in with you tomorrow. Right now I'm going up to Baton Rouge." She shut down Skype before Jada had anything more to say, then ignored her cell phone when Jada's ringtone sounded.

Gianna waited for her laptop to power down while grabbing some junk food to take on the road, most especially the beignets. She'd already unhitched her tent trailer from her cute little mini SUV, so all she had to do was throw her suitcase and backpack into the backseat.

She ran up the back walk to the kitchen and knocked on the door.

"Come in," Ophelia called out.

Gianna let herself in and smiled at the older woman. Gianna had liked Ophelia from the first day she'd met her, but after realizing what a support she had been to Sebastian growing up, Gianna now loved her.

"Did I see you throwing a suitcase in your car?" Ophelia asked as she wiped her hands off on a dishtowel.

Gianna glanced around the kitchen, disappointed that Sebastian wasn't there. Ophelia smirked when she saw Gianna looking. "Sebastian wasn't here when I got here this morning."

"Who says I was looking for Sebastian?" she asked, trying to look innocent.

"Gianna, I really like you, girl. I would hate to think that look of expectation on your face was for any of the other men in this house."

Gianna giggled. "You have a point."

"So, are you taking off to go somewhere?"

"I'm leaving for a couple of days to check out a couple

of artist studios, and I'll also do some sketching. I should be back before the week is out."

Ophelia stepped up to her and rested her hands on her shoulders. "In my day, young women did not go gallivanting all around the country by themselves without someone looking out for them. I don't like the idea of you being out there by yourself, Gianna."

Gianna giggled up at her. "Uhm, weren't you the one who told me that your aunt was a hippie and part of the flower generation and went to Woodstock?"

They both looked over as the kitchen door swung open. Gianna was able to mask her disappointment when it was Neil who walked through the door. "What's this about Woodstock?" he asked.

"Your wife was trying to make me think that twenty years ago was the nineteen forties, but she forgot she'd told me about her aunt attending Woodstock."

Neil came up behind his wife and put his arms around her and nuzzled her neck. "She's got you there, honey." Then his eyes narrowed as he looked at Gianna. "But what's going on with you? Is there something we should be concerned about?"

Gianna felt her heart melt. Neil and Ophelia were such good people.

"Nope, just going to do a little bit of traveling, checking out some of the local artisans and see if I can talk some of them to sell some things in my cousin's shop back in Kentucky. I'll also do some sketching."

"You check in with us every evening, you hear?" he said.

"I will."

Gianna gave them both hugs before heading out to her car.

It was time to do some sleuthing.

13

Gianna couldn't turn off her phone because she needed it for the navigation app, but all of Jada's incessant calls and texts were driving her batty. By the time she pulled into the Watermark hotel valet, she was ready for a glass of wine and a bath, and it wasn't even noon. Heck, was she turning into a wino?

It really ticked her off that she relied so heavily on Jada for everything when it came to computer snooping, because she really wanted to track down this Bradley Fontenot, and when she'd done a google search there had been a lot of them in Louisiana. Of course, she had his telephone number, but it wasn't like she could just call him up. Or could she?

She bit her thumbnail as she waited up in her hotel room for her luggage to be brought up. Her phone rang again. It was Jada. She let it go to voicemail. Then she got a text.

. . .

Just booked my ticket to New Orleans. Will be there tonight.

Oh no!

Gianna called Jada.

"Thought that would get your attention." Gianna could hear the smirk in her friend's voice.

"Did you really book your ticket?"

"Yep."

"I don't want you here. You have responsibilities at home. This is my issue."

"Gianna," Jada's voice was almost tender. "I don't doubt your abilities in the slightest. You are the strongest woman I know."

Gianna bit her lip as she sat down on the edge of the hotel bed. "You don't mean that."

"Yes, I do," Jada disagreed. "After the first month of rooming with you I figured things out, I realized you were the one with the backbone of steel. I was just the mouthy bitch who would throw down, but you were the real deal."

Gianna looked up and saw her reflection in the mirror over the dresser. The woman she saw didn't look too strong to her at the moment. "Sometimes it feels like it's all an act, and I'm that same little girl who was sitting on the floor of that dirty house when the police showed up. I feel lost and alone."

"But you're not. You inhale life. You don't let anything stop you. I hide behind my computer screen."

Gianna giggled. "That is the biggest load of horse pucky I've ever heard. You wouldn't own so many pairs of five-inch heels if you stayed hidden behind a computer screen."

"Okay, you might have a point," Jada agreed. "Now, where are you?"

"Baton Rouge."

"The state capitol. What are you thinking you can find, Little Miss Nancy Drew?"

"I want to track down Bradley Fontenot."

"So that's the guy's name."

Gianna giggled again. "Yep."

"I'm still pissed that you took that kind of risk by drugging Armand and digging through his phone. And you thought I was the strong one, *pfft*."

"I was fine," Gianna grinned. She knew that her friend's mama bear instincts would kick in, Jada just couldn't help herself.

"Well, you shouldn't have," Jada mumbled. "Okay, so what happened after you drugged Armand?"

"So I got his name and his number. I tried to track him down, but I haven't had much luck. There are a lot of Bradley, Brad, and B. Fontenots in Louisiana, and I haven't been able to find that phone number."

"And you didn't ask me to track it why?"

Gianna sniffed. "I wanted to do one damn thing on my own, okay?"

"But why?"

"It just felt like I couldn't do anything by myself, is all."

"Girl. You are pissing me off. We're a team. You know I want to help you figure out what happened to your mother. I've always wanted to help with that. How many times have you helped me when my life has turned to shit?"

Gianna slumped against the dresser. "I think that the whole Sebastian thing has kind of thrown me for a loop," she admitted.

She was met by dead air. "Jada, are you still there?"

"You really like him, don't you?"

"Yeah, I really do."

"Well, let's put that on the back burner. Right now we'll focus on finding out more about this Fontenot character. Do you really think he'll have something to do with your mom's death?"

"I really don't think so. I don't think Armand was part of it, I think it was Lazar. But this is the only thing I have right now, and I just have to do something," Gianna said with frustration.

"Okay, sunshine. Just know that I'm still following up on Rosie Ettabaum and I should be able to get you something on Bradley Fontenot soon."

"Thanks."

"You're welcome."

At least Dallas isn't as humid as Louisiana, Sebastian thought as he got out of the truck. They parked in the driveway of the small house in the Dallas suburb. Gideon knocked on the door and an attractive middle-aged Hispanic woman answered. She smiled up at them.

"Hello, gentlemen."

"Mrs. Lattimer, I'm Gideon Smith and this is my friend Sebastian Durand. I called you yesterday about some questions we had. Is now still a good time for us to visit?"

"I was expecting you." She smiled even wider. "Come in out of the heat."

Sebastian was a little surprised at how easily she accepted their presence in her home. As they followed her into the living room, she motioned for them to sit down. "I have cold sweet tea, lemonade, or beer, which would you like?"

Sebastian immediately noted the pictures on the shelves of three men in Marine uniforms. She saw his interest. "Those are my sons," she said proudly. "Only Alex is still serving. Randall and Derrick are both out and started their own construction company."

Well, that explained her ease with them.

"You're both in the Navy, that's correct, yes?"

"Yes, ma'am. We're stationed out of Virginia," Sebastian answered.

"So what can I get you boys to drink?"

"Lemonade is fine for me," Gideon responded.

"Same," Sebastian said.

She left the room and Sebastian continued to look around. There were a lot of pictures, a lot of family pictures. It looked like Mrs. Lattimer had a great life. That was really nice to see.

"Here you go." She placed the drinks on the coasters that were on the coffee table, then took a seat across from them. There was a glass of iced tea on the table beside her chair. "I had you come at this time so that we had a little privacy. Don't get me wrong, my husband knows what I did when I went to college, but still, I really don't like to talk about it in front of him if I don't have to."

Gideon took a sip of his drink and nodded. "That makes sense, ma'am."

"I really appreciate you answering these questions," Sebastian said.

"Now, your name is Sebastian Durand," she nodded her head at Sebastian. "I take it you're related to Lazar Durand, correct?"

Sebastian nodded. "He's my grandfather."

Her lips curled in distaste. "Yes, well, we can't always choose our relatives, now can we?"

"I take that to mean you've met my grandfather," Sebastian said.

"Yes, I've had the displeasure. Is this the reason for your visit?"

"Yes, it is."

Her hands that had been folded in her lap now moved to clutch the arms of her chair. "Do you have any specific questions?"

"There are a couple of things that I want to know. I don't think they're related. First, do you know if there is anything that my grandfather could have been doing that would have gotten him blackmailed?"

Her head tilted. "You mean besides the obvious, that he was paying for sex?" She sighed. "And before you ask. He was never one of my customers. He went for the blonde, blue-eyed girls, but I was hired for some of the parties that he hosted."

Sebastian gave her an easy smile, attempting to be both encouraging and sympathetic. Before he could ask a question, Gideon did.

"Can you tell us how those parties worked?"

"They were coordinated by Etta Rose. She would call us. She never left a voicemail, never sent a text or an e-mail." The woman took a small sip of her tea. "I liked the woman, I met her in person twice, I liked her. She was a sharp businesswoman, but also very kind. I never felt pressured."

Sebastian glanced over at Gideon, then back at Mrs. Lattimer. "How were you approached to work for her?" Sebastian asked.

"It was actually one of my sorority sisters who approached me. At the time it seemed like a miracle, because two weeks prior one of my larger grants had just fallen through."

"How did your sorority sister know about this? Had you told her?" Gideon asked.

"No, I hadn't. To this day I wondered how she knew the exact time to talk to me about the escort service. Only my parents knew about me losing the grant money, and how I wouldn't be able to attend the next semester."

"We actually think that somebody working with Etta Rose might have had access to financial aid, student loans, and needs-based scholarships and grants records," Gideon told her.

She took another sip of her tea, then nodded. "That would explain it. Like I said, Etta Rose seemed pretty savvy." She smiled at Sebastian and Gideon. "What else do you want to know?"

"So you were contacted for your assignments by telephone call? Was it Etta?"

"No, it wasn't Etta. It was a woman who always said she was calling on behalf of Etta. She never gave me her name. I always knew to pick up the call because the number always showed up as private, and when I star-sixty-nined them to get the number it never worked."

Sebastian and Gideon grinned.

"Etta's assistant would tell me the place and time I was to arrive, and who the client was. I always received money transferred into my account upfront. Usually, I worked twice a month."

"And Lazar?" Sebastian asked.

"I worked two parties for him. They were at a mansion on Highland Road in Baton Rouge, but for the life of me I couldn't remember anything more than that."

"That's just fine," Gideon assured her. "What can you tell us about the parties?"

"There were probably twelve girls hired for the night, but if I had to guess only three paired off with anyone. Instead, this was all about making the men feel like they were big deals."

Sebastian frowned, and she must have seen his expression.

"So we all arrived first. We were dressed in cocktail dresses, nothing too slutty. Our job was to, and I quote, act like ladies. There were no servers there, just Etta's girls and Lazar's guests. The caterers had left by the time we had arrived, the bar was all set up, so we served the food and drinks and made sure all the men felt high and mighty. It wasn't a real bed of roses, because there were about twenty of them, and they were all political types who kept having private conversations amongst themselves, so you had to know when it was appropriate to check in with them, and when to stay back. It was quite the balancing act."

"I bet it got worse as the booze started flowing," Sebastian sympathized.

"You got that right."

"Where was Lazar in all of this?" Sebastian asked.

"Oh, he was always in the great room, playing to an audience."

"Outside of the times with the parties, did you socialize with any of the girls? Did you hear of any of them having problems with Lazar?"

"I formed a casual friendship with one girl for a semester, but she never mentioned Lazar other than the party we attended together. We agreed we really didn't like him. Especially after we saw how he treated this one girl."

Gideon and Sebastian sat up straighter.

"What do you mean?"

"This is how Lori and I became friends. We'd gone to the bathroom together on the second floor, and when we came out, we heard shouting behind one of the bedroom doors. When Lori heard the definite sound of a slap and a girl crying out, she stormed into the room."

"What did you see?" Gideon asked.

"It was Lazar standing over one of us. She was lying on the ground. When he saw us, he pushed past us and went back downstairs." Mrs. Lattimer gave Sebastian a sad smile. "I'm sorry to have to tell you that about your granddaddy."

"I wish I could say I was surprised. How about you, were you ever hurt?"

"Nope. Never. That was the second and last party I ever did for him. When Lori and I asked Shelby what had happened, she said that she'd been sitting on some drunk asshole's lap while he and another man had been talking. Lazar came into the bedroom and went ballistic."

"Did she say who they were or what they were talking about?" Gideon asked.

"We didn't ask. We were more interested in what not to do to get in trouble."

"Got it," Gideon said. "Is that all the dealings you had with Lazar Durand?"

"Yes, it was."

Sebastian and Gideon stood up at the same time. "I really want to thank you for your time," Gideon said.

"You're welcome. I can't say that this was the happiest walk down memory lane, but I was hoping that since you were asking about Lazar that perhaps all of these questions might do something to end his political career."

Sebastian gave a half-smile. "That's something I'm hoping too, ma'am."

She gave a big smile.

"Oh, I have another question too, Mrs. Lattimer," Gideon said. "Do you have the contact information for your friend Lori?"

The woman shook her head. " I don't even know her last name. We just met up for coffee a couple of times. I've changed my phone number since then, so I don't have her in my contacts."

Sebastian held out his hand. "Well, thanks again."

She shook his hand. "You're very welcome, son." Then she shook Gideon's hand. "Please, both of you. Stay safe."

"We will, ma'am," Gideon said as they left her home.

14

When Jada had told her that Fontenot owned the Blonde Bayou and he was currently taking applications for waitresses, it seemed too good to be true. Jada had found some resume online and then made some adjustments to it so that Gianna could use it. Jada had also found Bradley's personal e-mail so that he'd get the resume immediately, along with a headshot of Gianna to entice him to interview her. That had been yesterday, and now here she was on the outskirts of Baton Rouge at a club with a parking lot that rivaled a Sam's Club.

As she started to wander around the club, Gianna looked at the waitresses and was amazed at their ability to stay upright as they balanced heavy trays of alcohol and gargantuan breasts, all on six-inch heels. There wasn't a chance in heck she would ever get a job here. She took a tour and realized that there were three dance floors and two different bars. The place was huge.

She walked up to one of the busy bars and squeezed her way through to the front. It took five minutes before one of the bartenders noticed her; that's what happened when you were short.

"What can I get you, honey?" the really handsome blonde bartender asked her.

"I'm here to see the owner about a job. A Mr. Fontenot."

He looked her up and down. "Honey, don't take this personally, but you don't have a chance in hell. You might want to skip it." His smile seemed a little off.

Gianna gave him wide eyes and her brightest smile. "I have a really good resume, and Mr. Fontenot said he would like to talk to me tonight."

He rolled his eyes. "Okay. Let me meet you at the end of the bar, and I'll show you where you need to go."

"Thank you so much." This time her smile was sincere.

Gianna had to bob and weave through a crush of people to get to the end of the bar, and by that time the blonde bartender was there waiting for her. He looked her up and down. "Well, you definitely have the curves for the job."

"Thanks," Gianna muttered.

"Okay, follow me."

She followed him to the hall that indicated the restrooms, and once again she found herself bobbing and weaving, but this time it was past the line of ladies who were waiting to go to the bathroom. At the end of the hall, there was a door with a keycard entry.

The blonde bartender swiped the card that he'd taken from his jeans pocket. "Brad's in the office at the top of the stairs."

"Thanks…" Gianna laughed. "I don't even know your name."

"Honey, no need to. You're not getting the job, you're not the type. Now if you want to come back to my place tonight we could maybe exchange first names. But no need for even that, come to think of it."

Gianna took a step backward. *It's amazing how fast handsome can turn to ugly*. Once again she gave him a big, innocent, fake smile. "That could be interesting, but alas, my boyfriend is expecting me home tonight."

"Your loss."

He turned and went back down the hall.

I need a shower.

She headed up the stairs. She wished she knew what she was getting into with Bradley Fontenot, but there hadn't been a lot of time for Jada to run a full background check on the man. He didn't have a police record, so that was promising. He and Armand were in the same graduating class from Louisiana State University. Other than that, nothing. Gianna took a deep breath, then knocked on the door.

"Come in."

She opened the door and stepped into the office, almost bumping into the belly of the huge man who was just inside the door. His beefy hands clamped down on her upper arms to steady her.

Oh, God.

"Well, there you are, sweet thing. Curtiss told me that he let you in. I've been looking forward to this meeting ever since I saw your picture."

"Mr. Fontenot," Gianna smiled brightly up at the man. "I can't believe how much you remind me of my father."

Fontenot's eyebrows shot up. "What?"

Gianna twisted her body, then dipped under his arms and walked over to one of the chairs in front of his desk. "Thank you for seeing me on such short notice. I really appreciate your kindness."

Gianna prayed that she was using all the trigger words

she could so that he would think of her more as someone to care for instead of someone to get all handsy with. She pulled the copy of her resume out of her purse, the one that she'd had the concierge at the Watermark Hotel print out for her, and put it on Fontenot's desk.

"How soon would you need me to start work?" she asked. Again she gave him her wide-eyed innocent look.

Fontenot stared at her for a moment, then he reluctantly crossed the room and moved behind his desk. He picked up her resume and scanned it. "Why don't you sit down?" he asked.

Gianna sat on the edge of the chair, her knees clamped shut and her purse tight on her lap. "Your establishment is really impressive. We don't have anything like this back home in Kentucky. How did you accomplish something like this?"

He picked up the pack of cigarettes that had been lying on the desk and shook one out. After he lit it, he leaned back and looked at her. "You're a long ways from home. What brought you to Louisiana?"

"My boyfriend." Gianna tried to think fast. "He just got out of the military and came back to be close to family. I came to be close to him."

"Last thing I need is for my waitresses to be bringing in jealous boyfriends and causing trouble," Fontenot said as he blew out a stream of smoke.

"My boyfriend wouldn't," Gianna assured him. Her eyes darted above his head to black and white photos of him shaking hands with different men. It reminded her of the photos that she'd seen in Lazar's office. "Who are they?" she asked as she pointed to the wall.

Fontenot turned his head to look back at what she was pointing at. He grinned back at her. "Those are some pretty important men. One of them's the governor." He stood up and rounded the desk, then leaned against the front so that he was towering over her. "Pretty impressive, isn't it?"

Gianna forced herself not to tremble. She hated him getting so close to her, but this was exactly the kind of information she'd been wanting, so she looked up at him and smiled. "The governor?"

"Yep," he leered down at her. "He and I did some business awhile back."

"You're involved in politics?" Gianna breathed out. "I've never met a politician before."

Fontenot laughed. "Sweet thing, I'm more honest than a politician. Now let's get back to your waitressing experience." He took another deep puff on his cigarette then blew it out, the stream of smoke hitting Gianna square in the face.

When she started to cough, he laughed again, then reached over and patted her on her back. Gianna arched away from his touch. "You're making me uncomfortable."

Fontenot pulled his hand away and gave her a piercing look. "Kind of touchy for some girl coming looking for a job, don't you think?"

"I'm just being honest, sir."

Fontenot shook his head and sat back down behind his desk. "Look, you're not waitress material for the Blonde Bayou." He picked up her resume, turned, and threw it in the waste bin behind him.

Darn, she really wanted more information. At the same time, she didn't want to be pawed. Gianna smiled timidly. "Do you have any other businesses where I might get a job?" she asked.

Fontenot rolled his eyes. "What makes you think I have other businesses?"

Gianna pointed to the pictures on the walls. "I just

thought if you had all of those friends, you probably did more than own this big bar, that's all."

She watched as a slow grin crossed his face. "Well, you're right about that, little lady." He rolled back his chair and grabbed her resume back out of the trash, then gave her another considering look.

"Besides waitress, what else can you do?"

"I'm good with the entire Microsoft suite of tools. I'm very organized. I've worked the front office in a dental office for six months."

Fontenot looked down at her resume. "Okay, I see that. Meet me here tomorrow at one o'clock and I'll take you over to my office in downtown Baton Rouge. There might be a position open for you there."

"Can't I just meet you there?" Gianna asked.

He glared at her. "You'll ride with me. Either take it or leave it."

She stood up and held out her hand. He grasped it. His big hand was huge and sweaty, and he held onto hers far too long. "We have a deal, Mr. Fontenot."

"Call me Bradley."

Sebastian was stretched in the bed next to Gideon's, watching the news with the volume off while his teammate worked at the little desk provided in the hotel room. The man dwarfed it.

Gideon growled, then started typing faster on his keyboard.

"Want to share with the class?" Sebastian asked, even though he continued to keep his eyes locked on the screen. The shit he was seeing made it obvious that they were soon going to be deployed.

"Fuck!"

Sebastian sat up higher on the bed, his gaze swinging between Gideon and the television. "What, are you seeing this?" Sebastian asked as he nodded to the T.V.

"Huh?" Gideon looked up from his computer and then glanced over at the television. "No, that's not it. I found more on your mother's death. It wasn't in the case files, but I found an e-mail between the investigating officer and his lieutenant. The lieutenant said to close the case, because it looked like two of the other murders they'd had the previous years. Both women had been stabbed to death."

Sebastian got off the bed and went around to look at Gideon's computer. "I can e-mail you their reports and you can read it off your goddamn phone because you don't have a tablet or laptop like any reasonable human being." Gideon scowled up at him.

"Jesus, untwist your panties. Let me read over your shoulder."

Sebastian quickly scanned the summaries of the two prostitutes who had been killed. Both of them had been teenage African American girls, and they had been stabbed repeatedly in their chest and abdomen and left in dumpsters.

"You have got to be fucking kidding me. My mother's throat was slit, and her body was found in a culvert outside of the city limits. These girls were found near the bus station. Was the lieutenant smoking crack?"

Gideon shot Sebastian a look. "You know what he was doing. He was following your grandfather's orders."

Sebastian slammed his fist down on the desk. "This gets us nowhere."

"Actually, there's more. The detective responded to his lieutenant. He said he didn't want to shut down his case, he had another lead he wanted to follow up on. Dumb bastard put it in writing. He was demoted a month later."

"We need to get his contact information."

Gideon grinned at Sebastian. "Already have it. Hope you weren't actually planning on getting some sleep tonight, because we're driving back to Baton Rouge instead of staying here in Dallas."

"You got that in one, because anyway, I'm sick of the way you drive," Sebastian said as he turned off the television. "You can sleep while I drive this time."

"It's my rental truck and I had to go out of my way to find that truck. I had to actually grease some palms."

"Quit your whining," Sebastian said as he got his shit out of the bathroom. "You know I'm the better driver."

"Bullshit," Gideon said as he closed his laptop with a laugh. "So tell me about Gianna."

Sebastian had been waiting for that question. "There's nothing to tell."

"Since you're going to be driving, I have hours to ask you questions. It will be fun."

Sebastian filled his duffel and glared at Gideon.

This so will not be fun.

15

"I've got your phone tracked, so keep it with you no matter what. Got it?"

"Jada, you're such a worry-wart," Gianna said as she walked toward the bar's entrance.

"I mean it. I don't like this. I couldn't find nearly as much as I would have liked on this guy, and it makes me nervous. How much battery do you have left on your phone?"

Gianna looked down at her phone and grimaced.

"Nine percent. But, but, but...I'll say it again. He backed off when I asked him to. It's going to be fine," Gianna assured her friend.

"I'm going to fucking beat your ass! Your phone is your lifeline."

"Look, I've got to go."

She tucked her phone into her purse, then walked into the bar. Even at twelve forty-five in the afternoon, it was hopping. When she got to the front of the bar, she was greeted by the same jerky bartender. He smiled at her. "I heard you made it for another round. You must have done something special up there."

"Actually, Mr. Fontenot is having me apply for a job other than as a waitress."

He sneered at her, "I bet he is. Come on, let me take you on up." Once again she pushed her way to the end of the bar and then followed him to the end of the hall so he could open the door that led her to Bradley Fontenot's office. This time Gianna did not engage with any more small talk.

When she knocked, Fontenot again called for her to come in, but she only opened the door, she did not walk in, afraid she would be once again met with him crowding her. Gianna was pleasantly surprised to see he was behind his desk. He was on his phone, waving her over to sit on one of the chairs in front of his desk. She sat down.

"Yeah, yeah, yeah. But you are not listening to me. I told you to get it fucking done now. You fuck this up, and I will personally see to you losing your license, your business, and everything you hold dear. You got it?" He paused. "I asked you if you fucking heard me, you piece of shit." He paused again. "Good. Now I'm sending Kevin over to make sure you deliver, expect him in an hour." He slammed down the phone.

Gianna did her best to not be upset by what she'd heard. Fontenot gave her a sly glance. "So, you think you can handle working for me, baby?"

She cleared her throat. "I don't actually know. What would I be doing?"

"That's what we're going to discuss." He picked up his pack of cigarettes and rounded his desk. "Let's go," he said as he grabbed her arm and pulled her out of her chair. She tried to shrug him off, but he didn't loosen his grip.

"Mr. Fontenot, please let go of me."

"One thing you're going to have to get used to is that I'm a hands-on guy. It doesn't mean anything. I open doors for women, and shit like that. Now let's get going." He opened the office door and pulled her down the stairs. If Gianna wasn't so intent on getting information about Armand out of the jerk, she wouldn't have put up with this, but she was sure she was on the right track. She could feel it in her bones.

When they got back into the bar area, people automatically parted to let him pass. Then they were outside and he threw on his sunglasses. "This way."

"My car's this way," Gianna pointed. "I'm going to follow you."

"I told you yesterday, you're driving with me. Trust me, you'll like it. I have a sweet ride. An Escalade. We need to go over a few things. My businesses are complicated, and I need to make sure you can handle them before I decide you're the right girl for the job." He tugged at her upper arm. "Come with me."

Gianna followed him, trying to keep her feet under her on the gravel parking lot in her heels.

When they got to the Escalade he opened the door for her. "See, like I told you, I open doors." When he got in and started the car he also pulled out a cigarette and started smoking. Gianna rolled down her window. "Jesus, how uptight are you?"

"Didn't you want to tell me about the job?"

"Right." He blew out smoke. "What do you want to know?"

"You said you had more than one business, what are they?"

He gave her a sideways glance. "I guess there's no harm in telling you now," he licked his lips and smiled. "I've done real well for myself. Real well. Started out with a pissant of a partner who fronted me some cash and connections. We went to school together, but he was dumb. He couldn't hold onto shit. He gambled on everything, cards, horses, ballgames, and investments. The dumbfuck lost every goddamn time. Meanwhile, I was smart. I made sure only to bet on a sure thing."

"Okay," Gianna said, stretching out the word. "It sounds like you really knew what you were doing."

"Damn fucking right I knew what I was doing. He didn't even know how to use the connections he had, dumb bastard. And with the father he had, you would have thought it would've been second nature. All you have to do is make sure that people like our old governor got a cut, and then you were set up."

Gianna shivered; he was talking about Armand. Why was he telling her this? This was bad. She looked over at him and saw he was concentrating on the road, so she slowly reached into her purse with one hand and grabbed her phone. She pulled it out just far enough so she could see it. He was making a left-hand turn so she pressed in her password, called up her recent call lists, and called Jada. She turned down her volume to zero and made sure to mute her phone. Just as Fontenot was turning his head she shoved her phone back in her purse, all the time praying that Jada had actually answered the phone and it hadn't gone to her voicemail.

"Mr. Fontenot, so what kind of businesses do you have, it sounds interesting?"

He sighed. "So you still want to play it that way, do you?" He was picking up speed.

"What are you talking about?" she asked nervously.

"You think you're smart, but I'm a whole hell of a lot smarter. I'm always the smartest man in the room. So don't give me that innocent shit now, sweet cheeks. I talked to

Armand yesterday. I know who you are. Here you show up with a phony resume asking questions. Once again he's the weak link bringing in a spy to the organization. Leaving me to take care of things."

"I'm not a spy," Gianna denied hotly.

"Bullshit. But you'll be able to make things right. I don't deserve what's happened to me. Armand's fucked me over, but at least he's found a way to make it right."

"What are you talking about?" Gianna felt her voice rising.

"I don't just own my club. It does all right, but new competition has come in and it's not bringing in as much as it used to. For years what's brought in the cash has been my private ambulance company. It was the biggest in three parishes until I had to use it to bail out my construction company, and all because of Armand's fuck-up."

When he didn't continue, she asked him a question. "What happened?" Anything to keep him talking. The car was going faster.

"I'll tell you what happened. Goddamned Armand Durand happened. I was stupid enough to listen to him. He told me that his dad had told him that a new annex to the state capitol was going to be built. Nobody knew anything about it yet, so my company would be on the ground floor on the bid. All I needed to do was make sure I was staffed and had all the supplies ready and I'd be a shoo-in. Took me six months to get my ducks in a row. Six fucking months, and I pulled in every favor I could and took loans out the ass. You want to know what happened then?"

"Okay."

"Turns out his old man was talking about the Mississippi state capitol building. How in the hell could Armand get that wrong? How? And I'm not even licensed to work in Mississippi."

Oh God, I'm in big trouble.

"What are you going to do to me?"

"Well, today is your lucky day." He grinned over at her as he got onto I-10 West. "Armand might be the world's biggest screw-up but occasionally he does have a plan that has a little bit of merit. We're going to use you as leverage."

Oh shit.

Gideon had gotten them a room at the La Quinta in Baton Rouge, and they'd just dumped their shit when Sebastian's phone rang with a number he didn't recognize so he let it go to voicemail. According to the info that Gideon had found, Reuban didn't get off his job as a security guard until four o'clock so they had a little time to rest and he needed a shower.

When a text came in, Sebastian glanced down at his phone.

S.O.S. this is Jada Harlow, Gianna's friend. She's been kidnapped. Call me.

Sebastian called the number, not knowing what to expect.

"Sebastian?"

"Yes."

"I'm conferencing you in to a phone call. It's kind of muffled, but you'll be able to hear what's going on. The man who has Gianna is named Bradley Fontenot and he's a friend of your uncle."

What the fuck?

"Gideon! Here, now!"

Sebastian put his phone on speaker and mute and placed it on his bed. He and Gideon both leaned over it as a click sounded. There was just a muffled sound of nothing. Gideon shot Sebastian a look. He looked down at his phone to ensure that mute was on.

"Jada, Gianna's friend, just conferenced us into Gianna's phone. She said Gianna's been kidnapped."

They had to wait for what seemed like forever before there was any kind of sound. "So where are you taking me?" a voice that Sebastian recognized as Gianna's asked.

"Don't worry about it," a man's voice answered. He had a strong Cajun accent.

"Well, I'm worried. It sounds like I'm going to be there awhile. Am I going to like it?"

"Jesus, you really are an uptight bitch, aren't you?"

"Well, am I?"

"She needs to shut up," Gideon murmured.

"That's not her style," Sebastian mumbled as he stared hard at the phone. But he so wished it was.

"Just shut up already! You're working my last nerve." This time his voice came through loud and clear.

"I'm just getting scared. Are you going to kill me?"

"Little girl, don't be stupid. I already told you, you're worth money. I'm leveraging your ass."

"But I'm not worth money. I mean, I have some, but not much. I'll need to go to the bank to access my savings account."

"I'm talking about the big payoff. The kid will pay for you. Armand saw you. Now keep your goddamn mouth shut!"

They ended up with dead air again and Gideon took three long steps to grab his laptop and started pulling up different windows. Sebastian didn't pay attention; he stared at his phone, willing Gianna to say something...

anything. He didn't know how long he was staring when he heard the distinctive sound of an incoming Skype call.

"Jada?" Gideon asked.

"Who are you?" Jada responded. "You're sure not Sebastian the fourth. Where is he?"

"I'm Gideon Smith, one of Sebastian's SEAL teammates." Gideon turned the computer so that Sebastian could be seen on-screen. "That's him. Sebastian, pick up the goddamn phone and get over here so we can talk to Jada."

The suggestion seemed to rouse Sebastian out of his fog. He picked up his phone and sat down on the bed beside Gideon, his focus now on the computer screen. "Thank you for helping Gianna," he said in a low voice.

"I haven't helped her yet. We have problems. I have the three-sixty app on my phone and it's connected to Gianna's phone, but my flighty friend had only nine percent battery life left at twelve-thirty central time. I have her tracked on I-10 West coming up on the 76 Interchange." Jada sucked in a deep breath. "I just don't know how much longer I'll be able to know where she is." Sebastian could see tears glistening in her big brown eyes.

"Jada, you've done well. Now, what else did you hear before you conferenced us in?" Gideon asked.

Shit, why didn't I think to ask that?

"The guy's name is Fontenot. He owns the Blonde Bayou, it's a bar. Gianna got his name off of Armand's phone when she drugged him."

Sebastian saw Gideon's jaw clench as he sent him a hard look. "She went up there to check him out. We arranged for her to interview with him as a waitress. He was a sleaze, but she figured she could handle it. That was yesterday. She went back today because he said he would get her another job with one of his other companies."

"Are you two stupid?" Sebastian cried out. "What the fuck were you thinking? And what the fuck was Gianna thinking getting in a car with some man connected with Armand that was a fucking sleaze?" he yelled. Then his glare jerked back to the phone that wasn't making any noise.

"Lay off, just because you're some kind of fucking super SEAL doesn't mean anything to me, you got it?" Jada's eyes sparked fire. "Do you want me to continue or not? Remember, Gianna's life is on the line, you swinging your dick is not helping."

"Jada, tell us what you know," Gideon said in a placating tone.

"Fontenot went on to tell her about all of his businesses. He owns part of a construction company that gets contracts with the Louisiana government, he owns part of an ambulance company. Armand has managed to screw up both of his companies, and he's pissed. Then Gianna tried to find out where he was taking her, but it didn't work. In the end, he said that Armand had an idea about how he could use Gianna as leverage." She stopped and took a breath.

"Then what?" Sebastian asked. He was more under control.

"That was the point I'd found your number and conferenced you in."

He glanced back at the phone, then at Jada. Ah God, her fear was palpable.

"You can help, right?"

"Yes. It's what we do."

As soon as he said it, he saw the conference call end, and his heart stopped. Gianna's battery must have died.

16

Gianna tried to keep calm, but she was shaking inside. After fifteen minutes of silence, she'd started talking again. She couldn't help it, plus she hoped that he'd tell her where they were headed, and maybe Jada could get help. He hadn't said a word; instead, she could just see his anger building, but she was desperate.

When he veered violently off onto the shoulder, she took her chance and grabbed at the door handle.

Her head slammed against the passenger side window. Pain like she'd never experienced before shot through her temple and Gianna slumped over. She heard rustling, but nothing made sense. All of her power was focused on trying to breathe…to stay conscious.

"You awake?"

She didn't answer. She didn't want to. All she wanted to do was leave. She lifted her hand to the handle and tried to pull at it so she could get out. She needed to get away.

"The door's locked."

"Awwwwww." She cried out as another sharp pain hit her ribs.

"Look down."

Gianna kept her eyes closed. She felt blood on her head and tasted it in her mouth.

"Look at my gun. Open your eyes and look at my gun."

How can he sound so normal?

Gianna kept her eyes closed.

Searing pain shot through her head again when he pulled her hair. "No. Please." Her words were slurred.

"How nice, begging. I like that from my bitches. But we don't have time. Look down and see the gun I have pressed in your ribs."

He shoved her head down and Gianna's eyelashes fluttered open. She saw the gun that was twisting into her side. It hurt. His finger was on the trigger. She was going to die.

"I told you to shut up. You didn't listen. Are you listening now?"

She opened her mouth, but no words came out.

He viciously yanked at her hair and she screamed.

"Are you listening?"

"Yes," she gasped.

"Good girl. Now I can drive in peace."

He slammed her head against the window and started the car. Gianna tried to think of something besides the pain, but she couldn't. When she opened her eyes to look out the windshield the sun shot a spear of light that was so bright it blinded her and she slid down in her seat, thankful when she succumbed to darkness.

"Where's he going?" Jada demanded.

Sebastian ignored her scared voice as he picked up his phone and demanded Gideon's keys to the truck.

"If I had to guess, he's going to find his uncle," Gideon said as he picked up his laptop and took it over to the desk. He fished his keys out of his pocket and handed them over to Sebastian.

"Why aren't you going with him?"

"We need to get to work."

"Gideon," Sebastian said as he got to the door. "Text me every pertinent cell phone number. I only have the landline to the house and Grandpère's cell."

Gideon nodded.

Sebastian shot out the door and called the landline at the Durand place, praying that Philly would answer. He was almost to the truck when the phone was picked up, and it was her. "Durand residence."

"Philly, it's me. Gianna's been kidnapped and Armand is behind it."

He was met by silence. Shit, he shouldn't have led with that. He should have just asked for Armand's phone number.

"I beg your pardon?"

"I'm pretty sure it goes back to Mom's murder." He unlocked the truck, swung in behind the wheel, and started the engine. It took more than a minute to connect to the Bluetooth.

Motherfucker!

"Philly, can you hear me?"

"I hear you. Let me get my mobile phone and get you his mobile number. Baby boy, this isn't really happening. This can't be happening." He heard the tremble in her voice. It was coming through the car speaker; at least the connection was working and that was a blessing. He had to think.

"Philly, any idea where Armand is?"

"Baton Rouge. He said he was going to use the family

apartment there, at least that's what I heard him tell your grandfather. But that's all I know." He heard a quiver. "That's all I know. I'm so sorry."

"Philly. It's all right. What's his number?"

As she rattled it off, he put it into his contacts. "You can't tell Lazar. You have to pretend everything is normal. Can I trust you to do that?"

He heard her blow out a breath. "But you need to tell the police."

"No. I need to take care of this. Now, what's the address to the apartment?"

She rattled that off as well as Armand's mobile number. "Baby boy, you have to go to the police. This isn't something you can do by yourself."

"I have a friend of mine in town. He's helping me. We'll get her back."

"Sebastian, wait a minute. I'm going to tell Neil. He'll help. This is your number, right?"

"Yes, just call me here. Thanks, Philly."

"I'll call you at this number if there is anything else that I think of, okay?"

"Thank you. Thank you so much." Sebastian listened to the phone disconnect, then stared out the windshield. He thought about Gianna out there somewhere, alone with that fucker. Scared. He saw his white knuckles gripping the steering wheel.

His phone rang. It was a Louisiana area code that he didn't recognize, but he'd bet anything it was Neil.

"Boy, it's me."

"Hey, Neil."

"Ophelia told me. Look, your uncle spends time at a club in Baton Rouge called the Leather Library. Been going there for years. It's some rich man's club. To hear him tell it he owns it, not damn likely in my opinion."

"Anything else?"

There was a pause and Sebastian would bet anything Neil was walking out of earshot of his wife.

"His favorite casino in Baton Rouge is L'Auberge, but I gotta tell you, that boy is a gambler, what with the horse track down in New Orleans and all the casinos there, I would have expected him to head east, not north. But if Ophelia says he was headed to Baton Rouge, you can take that to the bank, you know she's never wrong," Neil chuckled.

"Gotta go."

"Good luck."

Sebastian hung up and hit the navigation system to the Durand apartment. When he was on the road, he called Gideon and let him know what he'd found out.

Sebastian had to park a couple of blocks over from the apartments on Lafayette, then he had to wait twenty minutes before he could follow someone into the secured building. He was seeing red by the time he got to the apartment, but he tamped down his anger. He had to play this right in order to get Gianna home safe. He wanted the direct approach, but his gut was telling him to finesse the situation.

He rang the doorbell. There was no answer. When he knocked on the door, there still wasn't an answer. He looked up and down the hallway before pulling out his lock-pick tools. He made quick work of unlocking the door and let himself in. He didn't pay any attention to the high-end, modern décor, instead, he focused on the half-empty bottle of brandy on the kitchen island. He walked down the hall and looked in every open door. Every room was empty, but in the master, he saw clothes strewn all over the floor and across the unmade bed. He went through everything, looking for anything that might give him an idea of where he might be. All he found were a couple of twenty-dollar casino chips in one pants pocket for the L'Auberge Casino. Looked like Neil was spot on.

Sebastian looked at his watch. It was only sixteen hundred hours—wasn't it kind of early to be hitting a casino? Who knew, but it was the only lead he had.

A text came in. Gideon wanted him to call.

"Yeah?" he asked as he walked down the hall and sat down on the couch.

"Okay, I've sent you a preliminary background check on Bradly Fontenot. He's a legitimate businessman. He's a former president of the Baton Rouge Rotary Club."

"I don't give a shit."

"I understand that," Gideon said patiently. "But I want you to know who we're up against. There is nobody who is going to believe that this guy is in on a kidnapping. He grew up poor, he's out of St. Landry Parish in a little town called Krotz Springs. His family got into real trouble back when Fontenot was in high school. It was a huge scandal.

"What do you mean?"

"Well, three of his cousins were arrested for disposing of eleven thousand-fifty pound barrels of DDT in the Atchafalaya National Wildlife Refuge. It's forty-four thousand acres of swamp. This was back when he was seventeen. He was only a minor, but even the papers said that they were too stupid to have masterminded the scheme. None of the records that relate to the case mention Bradley Fontenot, but I find it interesting that the company that was fined millions for the clean-up eventually hired Bradley as a consultant when he graduated from LSU. I'm thinking that's not a coincidence."

Sebastian didn't think so either. "So he got into shady deals early."

"Absolutely."

Sebastian stared at the ugly painting on the wall, his mind seething.

"Shit, shit, motherfucking shit!"

"What?" Gideon barked out the question.

"He was headed West on I-10; that's straight towards the Atchafalaya swamp! If he's from around there, he could be stashing her anywhere." Dread dripped down Sebastian's spine.

"Where can I meet you?" Gideon asked quietly.

"I'm at Armand's apartment. But Armand isn't going to know where Gianna is." Sebastian grabbed at his hair at the back of his head and pulled. "Gideon, I need you to get as much information on Fontenot's family as possible. They're going to be key."

"I can have Jada work on that while I get to you."

"I don't fucking trust her! I fucking trust you!" Sebastian shouted into his phone.

"I need you to calm down. I'll be in contact with Jada the entire time. We need to be in the field together. Tell me the address to Armand's apartment."

Sebastian dragged in a breath then told him. "But I'm not waiting around for you. I'm heading over to the L'Auberge Casino. Armand is playing games that have at least twenty-dollar chips, so I'm going to head over to card games."

"Got it."

"But seriously, you need to look for Fontenot's family. They're the ones who are going to know where Gianna is."

17

"Cuz, she's got a nice ass."

Gianna whimpered as her head thumped against something hard. She was dizzy and when she opened her eyes it only made it worse. Muddy water and marsh splashed beneath her, and that was when she realized she was upside down and being carried over someone's shoulder. She could smell the distinct odor of methane gas that made her gag. The rotten egg smell was hideous. She'd caught whiffs of it before when she'd visited wetlands and swamps.

Gianna started gagging.

"Bitch, don't throw up on me!"

It was Fontenot.

She gagged louder, praying he would put her down. He let go of her and she crashed to the ground with a splash. Her hip hit some kind of rock as she landed and she screamed with the pain.

"Jesus, don't you ever stop bitching and whining?"

"Please let me go, Mr. Fontenot," Gianna begged.

He pushed at her with the toe of his boot.

"Ain't done with you yet," he smiled down at her.

Gianna panted, trying to keep herself from crying as she looked up at the three men surrounding her. She clamped her knees together and pulled down her dress.

"Ahhh, lookie, she's shy."

"Keep it in your pants, Darnell." Fontenot glared at the short, skinny man. "I need to make a video of her, so I can't have her damaged."

"We get to make a video?" The other man grinned wide. "You didn't tell us about no video. Sweet."

"Sweet Jesus, Linus, you lost even more smarts whilst you were in prison. How the fuck that was possible I do not know." Fontenot shook his head. "I told you the plan before. We're just stashing her for a few days, making a video each day, collecting some money, and letting her go. It's going to be easy."

"Bradley, don't be calling me stupid," Linus pulled out a knife. "I know what you's just said is a pile of shit. You're not going to be letting her go if she knows your name. You're killing her. So why can't we have fun with her?"

"Yeah," Darnell agreed.

Fontenot sighed. "We'll discuss this after we make the videos. I can't have them thinking that we're ruining the merchandise."

Gianna hadn't stopped staring up, her eyes darting among all three men. She'd never been so scared.

"Darnell, since you think her ass is so nice, you shouldn't mind a little mud. Pick her up so we can get to the shack."

"With pleasure."

Gianna cringed when the man yanked her up hard by her right arm.

"Owww."

He pulled her over his shoulder and cupped her ass. "Oh yeah, she feels real good."

Sebastian had been all over the main floor of the casino, twice. There was no sign of his uncle. He stepped out to the front entrance of the casino and called Gideon.

"Do you have a recent picture of Armand that you could text me?"

"I'm in a cab. Jada can get it for you."

"Fuck this. I don't want to talk to her. She was the one who helped Gianna get into this mess in the first place."

"Get over it, Durand. She's a source."

Sebastian's lips tightened. Gideon was right. "How soon will you get here?"

"I'm probably twenty minutes out."

"Good."

"Call her and don't be an asshole." Gideon hung up.

Sebastian looked down at his phone and found her number.

"Sebastian." Jada sounded relieved. "Have you found anything?"

"No." His words were clipped. He couldn't help it, he was too damned frustrated. "Look, I'm at Armand's favorite casino. I need a recent picture of him so I can show it around to see if anyone has seen him tonight. Can you send one to my phone?"

"Immediately. I'm also getting all of the information on Bradley Fontenot's family. I'll have everything by midnight. I promise." Sebastian could hear the fear in her voice. Gideon was right, he needed to stop being an asshole. Then he thought of something else she could help with.

"There are a couple of other things I need you to do."

"Anything. Name it. I need to get her back safe."

"After you figure out where Fontenot's family lives, I need you to see about getting some two-man airboats and some canoes to rent near where they live. I'm calling in some friends to help us search."

"On it. Anything else?"

"Armand's photo first."

"I've already texted it to you."

He looked down at his phone and smiled. Maybe she wasn't so bad after all.

"Thanks, Jada."

He went back to the casino and started cozying up with the different cocktail waitresses to see if any of them had seen Armand today. One of them suggested he go check out the high-limit poker game, so he wound his way through the casino and went up the stairs to the glass doors.

Shit, I need some kind of player's card to enter the room.

As he was walking back down the stairs, he saw another cocktail waitress on her way up.

He held up two twenty-dollar bills. "Do you have a moment?"

"Just a moment, hun. This tray is heavy and I've got some thirsty people in there."

Sebastian took the tray from her and she smiled. "Thanks."

He handed her the forty dollars and held up his mobile phone so she could see the picture of his uncle. "Is he in there?"

"Armand? Not today."

"You know him?" This was great fucking news.

"Sure," she smiled. "He's a big tipper, even when he isn't winning. Which is pretty much all the time. That man shouldn't gamble." She bit her lip, and Sebastian noticed she was kind of cute. "Don't tell anyone I said that, it's kind of against the rules for me to be saying someone shouldn't be gambling, you know?"

"Got it," Sebastian grinned. "Armand's my uncle. I'm Sebastian. My grandfather and I are worried about him. There's another hundred in it for you if you'd call me if he shows up."

She cocked her head and gave him a considering look. "Okay, what the hell."

He took his phone and handed her back her tray. He picked up the pen on her tray and one of the napkins and wrote down his number, then he pulled a hundred dollar bill out of his wallet and put it on her tray.

"Hey, I haven't called yet."

"I appreciate you looking out for me. I know you'll make the call if you see him."

She frowned. "You're too trusting for your own good, do you know that?"

"That is so not true. But right now, I'm thinking you're one of the good guys. I need a good guy." Sebastian started back down the stairs again.

"You just bet on the right girl. I am one of the good guys." Her smile was blinding.

Sebastian didn't know if it was the stress, the cigarette smoke, or the constant clanging of the slot machines that were giving him a headache, but he was relieved that he would be outside the casino entrance soon, and that was when Gideon texted that he'd arrived. He felt himself relax when he saw his friend through the glass door. Okay, things would get better now. When he was just about to push the door to go outside, he stopped and actually chuckled. Who knew he could chuckle, but this would do it.

Gideon had attracted female attention...again. There were three women in very, very, short skirts who had surrounded the man. It didn't matter that he was giving them his stone-faced look, they were doing their best to show off their cleavage and touch him with their long red and pink fingernails. He knew Gideon was uncomfortable as hell.

At last, something that was entertaining for the day.

The men of Omega Sky gave one another shit about their looks, their smarts, and their ability to pick up women, but Gideon Smith brushed all of that off. Yet, here he was being treated like a celebrity. He was a black man and an inch shorter than Sebastian, but a little broader in the chest, and Sebastian would bet money that one of the ladies had already commented on his cheekbones. They always talked about his cheekbones.

Sebastian laughed out loud when Gideon strode away and punched his phone.

He picked up the call.

"Where the fuck are you?"

"I'm sorry, I got distracted watching a show," Sebastian said.

"What are you talking about?" Gideon practically shouted. "A woman has been kidnapped and you're watching some woman taking off her clothes?"

Sebastian pushed the door and stepped outside. He lifted his hand. As soon as Gideon saw him, he gave him the finger and strode over to him.

"You think you're funny?"

"Hey, I needed a little bit of comic relief, so sue me." Sebastian looked over at the three women who were making their way over to them. "We better get to the truck before you get mobbed."

"Fuck you, Durand."

When they got to the truck, Gideon asked what was next.

"I'm thinking the Leather Library," he said, and he started the engine.

"Hold up," Gideon said. "We're not dressed for it."

"And how do you know?" Sebastian asked as he started to make his way out of the parking lot.

"I'm research, right? That place actually has a dress code. No jeans and a tie is required."

Sebastian clenched his teeth. "Fine, let's hit a mall."

Gideon found a location for a mall and punched the address into the navigation system. Sebastian did the best he could to keep his speed under the speed limit, but it was tough.

"I'm going to make a call while we're driving. At least that will seem more productive."

Gideon was looking down at his own phone when he nodded.

Philly's voice came on the line through the truck's Bluetooth.

"Sebastian, have you found her?"

"Not yet, Philly. I need to talk to Neil."

"He's in our backyard. Let me get him."

Sebastian realized that never in his life had he been to Ophelia and Neil's house. There had been plenty of times that Philly had spent the night at the Durand house to take care of him if he'd been sick or something, but never had he been to the Heberts' home.

"Thanks, Philly."

He continued to follow the navigation system through the streets of Baton Rouge, then he heard Neil's voice.

"What do you need, son?"

"The man who has taken Gianna used to live in Landry Parish, right near the Atchafalaya Swamp."

"And you think that's where he's going to take her?"

"He was heading west on I-10 out of Baton Rouge."

"Okay, I see your point. But, son, you won't just be able to go out there and find her. It's too big," Neil whispered.

"I know that. We're finding out who his people are. One way or another, they'll tell us something."

"Okay. Okay. What do you need?"

"Even if we have a direction to go in, we are still going to be in trouble, unless we have one of them leading us right to her."

"Do you think that's likely?"

"I don't know, Neil. Maybe. But if we only get pointed in the right direction, I'm going to need some trackers with me and Gideon. People I trust. People who know the bayou."

"People like Fergus and Callum," Neil said.

"Exactly."

"I'll start rounding them up, boy. We'll head up your way. You give us a meeting spot."

"It won't be tonight. Hopefully tomorrow. But keep them on standby."

"Will do."

18

"Wake up!"

Gianna heard something, but it didn't make sense.

"Wake up!"

Pain shot through her upper arms, and her body shook. Pain speared through her head.

"Wake up!"

Water exploded across her face. "Ahhhhhhh. Stop," she pleaded. When she lifted her lashes, water dripped into her eyes so she slammed them shut. She tried to rub her eyes but someone's hands held her arms so she couldn't.

"What's happening?"

"Get her cleaned up. We need to start the video," a familiar voice spoke.

Something rough scrubbed her face and she started to cry; the pain was excruciating. "Please stop," she begged.

It was a towel. When she realized her arms were loose, she tried to push him away when he started to rub her hair. "Stay still or I'll hit you," he growled.

Gianna opened her eyes again. She could barely make out anything in the dim light. Then someone sparked a flame, and she saw Bradley Fontenot's face while he lit a cigarette. He was watching her dispassionately.

"Be sure to get off all of the blood and mud, I need them to be able to clearly see her face."

She remembered now. They were going to make a video and then kill her. Gianna started to tremble. It got so bad that she listed, and would have fallen off the chair if the man drying her hadn't shoved her back on it.

"Brad, she can't sit up," the man said. "I'm not sure she can do the video."

"I don't care if we have to do it with her lying on the floor. We need to give them the first one tonight. Got it?"

First one. Thank God. They were going to do more than one. I still have a chance to live.

"How's that?"

Fontenot walked over to her, bent down, and grabbed her by the chin, forcing her head up. "Not good enough." Gianna saw him reach down to the floor, pick up a bottle of water, and open it. He poured it over her head.

"Goddammit, that was my only dry towel," the other man complained.

"Use your shirt."

Gianna was able to sit upright in the hardback chair as the tall, skinny man stepped back and pulled off his shirt, then he threw it over her head. She gagged at the overpowering smell of body odor. He rubbed the foul-smelling cloth all over her head, making her eyes water. She tried to get away from him, but she couldn't. Finally, he ripped the rank shirt away.

"There, does that meet with your approval?"

"It'll do," Fontenot said as he threw down his cigarette.

He pulled a phone out of his back pocket and fiddled with it.

"That's not your phone," the skinny guy said.

"Of course it's not," another voice chimed in. That's when Gianna realized there was someone else in the room. "Our cuz wouldn't use his real phone; that could get traced back to him. You really are a stupid fuck."

"Both of you shut up. I need to concentrate. I need to make sure the flash is working." Fontenot was still looking down at his phone and Gianna was desperately trying to think of something to say or do. Anything.

"Got it." Fontenot looked up at her and grinned. "Here's what we're going to do. You're going to tell lover boy that he needs to cough up five million, or you die. How Armand explains it, it'll take a few days for him to get access to it, but after he does, Armand will give him wiring instructions. You tell him I won't hurt you, and I'll let you go."

"I don't have a lover," Gianna protested. "And I don't know anybody who has that kind of money."

How badly did I hurt my head?

"You didn't seem that stupid in my office," Fontenot muttered. "And it better be that you're stupid and not that fucking Armand got something wrong again."

Gianna cringed at the anger in Fontenot's voice.

"Lazar's grandson. Sebastian the tenth or whatever the fuck he is. The soldier. He's got the hots for you, right?"

Gianna slowly nodded then whimpered as pain lanced through her head.

"Quit your bellyaching, do you understand me?"

She hoped she did. Maybe Sebastian liked her enough to come to her rescue. She swallowed back tears. Was it too much to hope for, that Sebastian might notice her gone and want to come for her?

"Well, okay, Armand got something right," Fontenot laughed. "Armand showed me the real will, so at least I know that the kid has money coming to him from his great-grandfather. Lazar's just worked a deal with the family lawyer to cheat him out of it. That's why it's going to take a few days for him to get his hands on the five million, but Armand has a way to help. If he doesn't, I'll kill him."

Sebastian had five million dollars? Fontenot was going to kill me and *Armand?*

Gianna was so dizzy she thought she was going to throw up. She couldn't make sense of anything.

"So you get ready to tell your boyfriend that he has to pony up the five million if he wants to see you alive. You tell him he has to work with Armand to get the money and that Armand will know how to get the money to me. Got it?"

Gianna didn't nod this time, she whispered, "Yes."

Fontenot held up his phone. "Smile and talk. If you mention my name I'll let my cousin take a turn at you. Do you know what I'm saying?"

"Please say his name. Pretty please," the man she remembered as Darnell said.

"Now, action."

Gianna stared at the phone. "Sebastian, it's me, Gianna. I did something stupid and now somebody has me. He wants a lot of money from you and he says he'll let me go if you give it to him…I mean to your uncle."

"Five million," Fontenot whispered.

"He needs five million dollars," she gulped. She started to cry. "He says your uncle will help you get the money, and then you have to give it to him." She used her sleeve to wipe her nose.

"You're done," Fontenot said as he lowered the phone. "Not too bad." He looked over his shoulder. "Tie her up. If one of you comes back here without me, I'll kill you. You got me?"

Gianna looked at the skinny one and Darnell. She prayed that they were frightened. She prayed hard.

Sebastian's heart leaped into his throat when he saw the text with the video attachment. Gideon looked over at him. He tilted his phone so his friend could see.

"Open it."

They'd just dumped their shopping bags in the back of the truck.

"Once we're inside the truck," Sebastian muttered. He opened the door and got behind the wheel. He knew what this was. He knew down deep in his bones and only his training was allowing him to keep it together.

When both of their doors were closed, he pulled up the file. The video was shit. Gianna's face was grainy, but there was no mistaking her fear. Her eyes were pleading.

"Sebastian, it's me, Gianna."

Jesus, he felt that those words down to the bottom of his heart.

"I did something stupid and now somebody has me. He wants a lot of money from you and he says he'll let me go if you give it to him...I mean to your uncle."

He heard somebody whisper something, but he couldn't make it out.

"He needs five million dollars."

Gianna started to cry. Sebastian wanted to crawl into his phone and comfort her.

"He says your uncle will help you get the money, and then you have to give it to him." She used her sleeve to wipe her nose.

The video ended.

"What the ever-loving-fuck!" he roared. "What the fuck

is she talking about?" He slammed his hands against the steering wheel.

His uncle?

He drew back his fist.

"Fuck you!" he roared at Gideon when the man grabbed his arm, stopping him from punching the windshield.

"Calm your shit down!"

"Did you hear her? Armand? What is going on?" He tried to get his breathing under control.

"Calm." Gideon stared at Sebastian with compassionate eyes. "Calm."

"How can my family be even more depraved? I don't get it, Gideon. I don't. How deep does the rot go?"

Gideon let go of his arm and Sebastian looked away from him, taking three deep breaths. This was not helping things.

His phone had dropped to the floor of the truck, so he picked it up. He swiped in his password and texted Armand. He probably should have done that from the get-go.

Your friend Fontenot has Gianna. Says you can help me put my hands on five million, and you're the go-between. Call me.

He knew Gideon had been reading over his shoulder.

"Is that calm enough for you?" Sebastian asked.

Gideon nodded. "Sebastian, do you have the slightest idea why Fontenot thinks you can get your hands on five million dollars?"

"Hell no. It sure as hell isn't from my checking or savings account. Lazar has money, but until he dies none of it is coming my way. Fuck, to tell you the truth, even when he does die I'm not expecting one red cent. So unless Armand has some way for me to kill Armand and get my inheritance in a couple of days, or get a loan from Armand, which isn't fucking likely, then I don't know what is going on."

"Let's get to the apartment and get changed. We can discuss our next steps."

Sebastian nodded. There was nothing new about Gideon being the calm one, and God knew he needed it right now. He started the engine and headed toward Lafayette Avenue.

"We've got a couple of different things we're working on," Gideon said. "Two you know about, one you don't."

Sebastian glanced sideways at his teammate. "Start with the one I don't know about."

"Armand's cell phone provider is the rinkiest dinkiest Podunk provider I've ever heard of. Why the hell he's using it, is beyond me. Jada is trying to get into the system so we can set up some way of tracking the phone."

Sebastian glowered at Gideon. "Why the fuck aren't you doing it?"

"Again. Calm your shit down. She's doing everything I would be doing."

"Bullshit, you would have found a way to track him already."

"No, I wouldn't have. Now, number two. She's already sent me some of the stuff on Fontenot's family. They've reproduced like rabbits. The most interesting thing is that two of his three cousins, who got sent to prison for the chemical dumping, are out. They moved back to Landry Parish."

"Then we start with them."

"I agree," Sebastian said.

"Next, we need to find Bradley Fontenot. Jada's sent me

his home address and where his ex-wife lives. Apparently where he spends most of his time is the Blonde Bayou."

"You don't think he'd be stupid enough to show up there, do you? Wouldn't he be hiding under a rock?" Sebastian asked.

"I think he is one cocky son-of-a-bitch who probably thinks he can either pin this on one of his cousins again or Armand. He doesn't know what I know."

"And what's that?" Sebastian asked.

"Jada recorded that entire phone conversation between him and Gianna in the car."

"Holy shit. I've changed my mind. I really like her."

19

Gideon had arranged a room for the six men and Neil, who had arrived at the La Quinta Inn, and now they were all down for the night. It had been a long day and night, with nothing to show for it. They'd gone to the Blonde Bayou, the Leather Library, Bradley Fontenot's house and visited his ex-wife and gotten nowhere. What's more, his damned uncle hadn't responded to any texts or phone calls.

Sebastian pulled out his phone.

"What are you doing?" Gideon asked as he looked up from his laptop.

"Calling dear old Grandpère."

Sebastian didn't have to wait long. "Where the fuck are you? Everybody had to leave, and you've left a piss-poor impression. Do you know what it's going to take to cover your ass?"

"I need you to get Armand on the line and tell me where he is. I need to see him tonight."

"We have a campaign to run. I've already spent a half-million dollars of my own personal money on this. These boys are the movers and shakers of Louisiana politics; you can't do shit in this state without their say-so, and you're fucking it up. Now you're going to have to pucker up."

"Get my fucking uncle on the phone and tell him to meet me at the Baton Rouge apartment in an hour."

"Listen to me, you little cocksucker. Don't you take that tone with me. I own your ass. You will do what I say, when I say it. Get your ass back home now, and be ready to work."

"Old man," Sebastian said quietly between gritted teeth. "I'm not some call girl you can beat and get rid of. You had better listen to me when I talk to you. If you want one ounce of my cooperation, you will have your stupid, drunken asshole of a son at the Lafayette Avenue apartments in one hour."

"What are you talking about, some call girl?" Sebastian heard the slight thread of apprehension in his grandfather's voice.

Good.

"Are you listening to me? Make the call. Get Armand there."

He hung up.

Gideon snorted. "I take it we're heading out?"

"Yep."

"I really would have wished you'd put that on speaker. I could hear a little bit of how he was talking to you, but not all of it. He's got a colorful way of talking."

"Yeah, he's a smooth talker all right. Must be why he gets so many votes." Sebastian grimaced. "Ready to head out?"

Gideon nodded. He shut his computer and put it into his backpack. They headed out to the truck and were soon on their way. "Do you think your uncle will be at the apartment?"

"My uncle is scared shitless of my grandfather, and I was a horse's ass for not calling Grandpère from the get-go," Sebastian sighed. "We might have to wait for a bit. I'm not sure he'll be there within an hour, but the asshole will definitely show up."

"You sure do have a colorful family, Durand."

"Yeah, I'm lucky."

Sebastian figured he was due for some luck when they found a parking spot across the street from the apartment building. Still, they did have to wait about the same amount of time as last time before they could follow someone into the secure building. When they got up to the correct floor, Sebastian took out his lock-pick set.

"A gift from Landon?" Gideon asked.

"What do you think?" Sebastian asked as he let them inside.

He looked around the apartment. Nothing had been touched since the last time he'd been inside, the bottle of brandy was still at the same level. He walked to the master bedroom. All of the same clothes were where Armand had left them.

"He's a slob," Gideon said.

"Wish that was the worst thing I could say about my uncle."

Sebastian followed Gideon back down the hall and watched him open up the refrigerator.

"Did Armand go grocery shopping?" Gideon wanted to know.

"Probably the concierge service."

Gideon pulled out cold cuts. "I'm going to make us sandwiches."

"Whatever."

Sebastian sat down on the couch and called up Gianna's

video on his phone. He kept it on mute as he watched for the fifth time. Each time was worse.

"Hey!" Sebastian exclaimed when Gideon pulled his phone out of his hands.

"Here. Eat." His friend handed him a plate with a sandwich on it. "Armand might be here soon."

Gideon was right. Sebastian took the plate and dug in.

"Why'd you come to Louisiana anyway?" Sebastian asked. "I've been meaning to ask you."

"You never came back home before and I knew what happened with your mom and dad."

Gideon took a bite of his sandwich and swallowed. "When I talked to you, I have never heard your rage so close to the surface, and we've been in some hideous situations. I was worried."

Sebastian tightened his lips. He hated this. Relying on teammates when they were on a mission was one thing, but during a personal situation?

"Fuck, Durand," Gideon shot up out of his seat, practically throwing his plate on the coffee table. "You're one fucked up fool, you know that?"

What was Gideon talking about? Sebastian didn't respond, just waited for the man to have his say.

"Kostya wanted to come too, did you know that?"

Sebastian's spine went stiff.

My lieutenant wanted to come to Louisiana?

"Your family was so fucked up that you still haven't even figured out how friends work. You're going to have to figure this shit out, and fast. We're not just your teammates on a fucking mission, we're your teammates, your friends, and your brothers all the goddamn time. We have your back in all aspects of your life. And if you don't understand how that shit works, you're going to fuck it up with the woman that is taking up your entire headspace."

Sebastian threw down his plate then grabbed the hair at the back of his head. "What are you talking about? Gianna?"

"Give the man a cigar," Gideon growled at him. "Sebastian, the entire time I've known you, except for the members of Omega Sky, you've had no real emotional attachments, and that's because you've been fucked in the head by your family. But I didn't know it was so bad that you wouldn't understand that your brothers wouldn't want to help you outside of a mission."

Sebastian felt something akin to panic choking him. "That's not true, I'm attached to Philly and Neil."

"The Heberts? The people who care for the house where you grew up? How come I've never once heard of them? Have you ever been in contact with them since you left Louisiana?"

Sebastian tried to swallow but was having a hard time.

"Exactly. I didn't think so. Man, you're shut tighter than a mummy's tomb. You gotta stop it. You gotta know there are people you can trust outside of work, and you gotta let people in. Now excuse me, I gotta take a piss."

Sebastian watched Gideon as he stomped down the hall. He felt like he'd just been through a meatgrinder. He got up and looked in the fridge. He found a beer and took it out onto the deck, then leaned back where he could see the entrance to the apartment. He spied his phone on the coffee table, but he didn't have the energy to go get it. It didn't matter, he needed a minute to think.

Hell, I need a month to think.

He took a pull from his beer.

Am I really that emotionally closed off?

His jaw clenched. What in the hell was Gideon thinking going at him like that? Gianna had been kidnapped, and she could end up dead. Really? Was now really the time to be throwing down some bullshit psycho-analysis?

Sebastian looked at his phone again. His fingers itched to grab it and watch the video again; he desperately needed to see Gianna's face. What was happening to her right now?

He took another long sip of beer.

Why do I care? I've never cared about a woman so much, and I barely know her.

He watched as Gideon pulled his computer out of his backpack and wondered what he was working on now. The man was always working on something. How much did he really know about Gideon anyway? He'd met his family, and he really thought they were good friends, but after what he'd just said, did he really know him?

"Fuck!"

He took another pull from his beer, frustrated when he realized it was empty. Where in the hell was Armand? How was he going to get five million dollars to ransom Gianna?

His stomach churned, the roast beef and beer were not sitting well.

The couch was damp and it smelled like urine. Gianna had tried to wiggle her hands enough to get the ropes off her wrists, but the last time she did she'd almost fallen off the couch. As much as she hated the piss-smelling sofa, it was better than sleeping on the floor. Once again she hoisted herself up into a sitting position, swinging her legs over the side of the couch, and looked around the tiny cabin. She could only see a few feet in front of her.

"Shack. Admit it, it's a swamp shack."

Bugs that kept flying around her face and she couldn't

do anything to swat them away, and then there were all the spooky sounds that kept coming from outside. She itched from her million bug bites, and her head and hip hurt like crazy. She'd been talking out loud for hours, trying to keep herself calm, strong, and sane. She was pretty sure it wasn't working.

"Ummm."

She clamped her lips shut, mad that she'd let out a sob.

"Gianna Fawn Prentiss, don't you dare cry!" she yelled into the darkness.

She yanked at the ropes that were holding her wrists tight behind her back. She yanked, and yanked, and yanked. This time when she started crying at least it was for a good reason; the burning pain in her wrists was hideous, and she could feel the blood dripping down her hands onto her fingers.

"Shhhhh. It's going to be all right. Bradley's not going to kill you yet. He still needs you." She rolled her eyes heavenwards. It had happened, she'd lost her mind. She was trying to soothe herself like she was a baby.

She gasped, then brought her feet back up on the couch, trying to huddle into a ball. She heard another sound, different than any of the others. Was that what an alligator sounded like? Her pulse was beating so hard in her temples she thought her head would split open. Gianna heard scraping, or was it clawing? A dim shaft of moonlight was coming from across the room, but not enough for her to see anything, just a little bit that told her the cabin door had opened. She heard claws tapping against the floorboards and she screamed. She screamed like her life depended on it.

20

As soon as the apartment doorknob turned, Sebastian was across the room. He flung the door open and yanked his uncle inside by his shirt.

"What?!" Armand choked out as he started to struggle.

Sebastian slammed the door shut and shoved the man to his knees. "Talk."

"Bastian? Is that you, boy?"

Out of the corner of his eye, he saw that Gideon was still at his computer, calmly watching what he was doing.

"You saw my text. I saw that it was read." Sebastian was so many levels beyond pissed.

Armand looked frantically around the apartment, his gaze resting a minute on Gideon before focusing on Sebastian. He licked his lips. "Yes. Yes, I did, Bastian. I got your text. That's why I'm here, son. I'm here to help."

Sebastian squeezed the back of his uncle's neck, cringing as the man's greasy hair slithered over his hand. "I am, I'm here to help," he said again.

Sebastian squeezed harder. "Try again."

"What do you want me to say?" Now there was a pleading tone in his voice.

"I know you're in it with Bradley Fontenot. I know you're his partner. Now he has Gianna and he thinks you can get me to pony up five million dollars. I'd offer to trade your ass for her, but I think he'd prefer to cut off your dick and shove it down your throat before he'd give me Gianna. The man wants his money, and you and I both know you don't have it. So what the fuck is going on?" Sebastian squeezed so tight that Armand squealed with pain. The only thing keeping him upright was Sebastian's hold.

"I can't think," Armand wailed.

"Try."

Armand started to cry. "It's not just Bradley. I owe a lot of people. They're all out for blood."

"Like I give a fuck. Get your daddy to bail you out."

"He won't this time. I need *your* money."

Armand started to cough and wheeze so Sebastian let him drop to the floor. He looked over at Gideon and shook his head. Then he looked back down at Armand and kicked him over onto his back. "I don't have any money, you dumb bastard." Sebastian bent down and patted down his pockets, pulling out his cell phone. He threw it over to Gideon who caught it. "Now tell me where Gianna is."

"I don't know," he whined.

"That's a goddamned lie. On the video, Gianna said you're the go-between. You know where she is. You're in on this."

"I don't know where Gianna is, and you do have money. Your dad and I both got money from Sebastian the first, our grandfather. It went into a trust and we got it when we reached the age of twenty-one. When your daddy died, your grandfather was the conservator of your money until you reached twenty-one, but after you cut ties, he had the family attorney do some finagling and somehow got it put over into his name."

"You're more drunk than usual," Sebastian spit out.

"It's true. It's all true. I checked the balances, there's at least eighteen million. More than enough to pay off Fontenot and the others."

Sebastian stared down at his uncle. The man just lay there; he was so pathetic that he didn't even try to pick himself up off the floor—what kind of man was he?

"If what you're saying is true, why do you think Sebastian will use his money to pay off your other debts?" Gideon asked as he stepped up beside Sebastian.

"Bastian won't know what accounts to look at or where the real paperwork is. I do." The sly look on Armand's face made Sebastian want to puke.

"I'll be able to find it," Sebastian assured him.

"Yeah, but not in time to rescue your little piece of tail." Armand rolled over and got on his hands and knees as he attempted to push himself off the floor. Sebastian kicked him in the ribs and he flew over onto his back with a gasp. "Why'd you do that?"

"Because a miserable piece of shit like you deserves to stay on the floor." Sebastian turned to Gideon. "Do you think you can access what Armand is talking about, so I don't have to do business with him?"

Gideon gave Armand a withering glance, then looked back up at his friend. "Let me see what I can find out tonight. If I don't have any luck by morning, we'll be stuck using him."

"You'll need me. You'll see."

This time Armand tried sitting up. Sebastian and Gideon just walked away in disgust. Sebastian watched out of the corner of his eye as Armand got up and went over to the bottle of brandy and poured himself a hefty glass.

"You're going to be pretty thankful for your dear old uncle when you come into all of this money," he smiled as he raised his glass.

Was the man stupid? Had the booze really turned his brain to Swiss cheese? How could he think he would give him any money for his debts? Hell, there was very little chance he was going to pay Fontenot, because that would just ensure that Gianna would end up dead. Both of those men needed to end up behind bars, or worse.

"Sebastian," Gideon whispered from where he was sitting. He pointed down at his computer. There was a list of Fontenot addresses on the screen. A long list. All of the addresses were in Landry Parish. They were fucked.

Sebastian sat down beside Gideon on the couch, still keeping an eye on his uncle while he stood there drinking in the kitchen. "Jada's putting together a quick family tree, so we can determine who's closest to Bradley. The names highlighted on the list are the cousins, his mother, father, two sisters, and his brother."

Sebastian nodded.

"I'm having her put together any properties that aren't in Krotz Springs city proper. Those might give us an idea of where they might be hiding her. I was going to do it, but instead, I'll work on your family trust and the accounts."

"Gideon, how fast could my grandfather move this money out of the country?"

"Why?"

"I want to go pay him a visit tonight."

Gideon nodded. "I could see how you would want to do that. But he could have all of it moved to an offshore account in hours if he has one set up. It's better to wait until the accounts are frozen."

"Can you freeze them?"

Gideon slowly grinned. "When the bank opens on Monday, I can make that happen."

Sebastian's fists clenched. He'd have to wait thirty-six hours before he could confront his grandfather.

After her screams last night, Gianna had passed out. When she had woken up in the dark, she'd prayed for what seemed like a lifetime before dawn broke. Light slowly crawled over the cabin floor and she peered intently into the far corner where she had last heard the sound of claws tapping. No matter what, she promised herself she was going to keep calm.

She watched as the dust motes floated in the air and the light continued to creep across the dirty floor.

Gianna gasped when the raccoon shook itself, then sat back down and curled up on the tarp.

For the love of God. A raccoon?

Her lip quivered and she sucked in a deep gulp of air. It was helping as she felt her nose tingle. Tears slipped down her cheeks. She rubbed her face against her shoulder, not caring that it hurt to move, just wanting to wipe her face and not feel like the coward she was.

She jerked upright.

That sudden movement hurt too, but not nearly as much as the word she'd just used to describe herself.

Coward?

Never in her life had she ever thought she was a coward. Not even when she went to NYU and Jada thought she needed to be protected. Yeah, she might have been naïve, but never a coward. A person couldn't have a childhood like she'd had and be a coward, and she sure as fucking hell wouldn't allow herself to think she was one now.

She inspected the entire cabin. Granted, her hands were tied right now, but they might not always be, and when they weren't, she'd need a way to fight or escape. It was about time that she started to pull up her granny panties and figured out a way to rescue herself.

The raccoon got up and started to waddle toward her.

"What do you want?" Her voice was surly.

His head cocked at the sound of her voice.

"Don't mess with me today. I'm not in the damned mood. You got that?"

He took another step toward her.

"Out!" she shouted.

He jumped.

"I said get the hell out of here!" she shouted again.

The raccoon scurried out the door.

"You're not going to have all the fun," Fergus shouted.

"Damn right," Callum bellowed. "If you intend to ask these cousins some questions, we want to be there."

Sebastian covered his mouth, trying not to laugh.

"Men, we just need you for the search. Sebastian and I will get the answers we need," Gideon assured him.

Callum started laughing. "These are swamp boys. Are you willing to go the distance?"

"Trust me, Fergus, we'll take care of it," Gideon smiled easily.

"I'm Callum."

"Gideon, we're taking the O'Malley brothers with us," Sebastian interrupted. Gideon scowled at him. Sebastian knew that the bayou boys would end up being a hell of a lot more scared of the O'Malleys than they would be of some Navy SEALs. It shouldn't be that way, but it just was, Gideon would end up understanding.

"We'll follow you out there. That way when the search starts, we'll be close," Neil said, indicating him and the rest of the men.

Sebastian nodded. They needed to get moving. It was Sunday morning, and they didn't have any time to waste. It had been clear after talking to Armand last night that he knew nothing about anything. His only concern had been trying to ensure that nobody killed him. Why in the hell he was still going out to clubs was one of life's biggest mysteries.

When they got into the truck and started west on I-10 with all of the others following them, Gideon connected his phone with the truck's Bluetooth and made a call.

"What took you so damn long to call?" Jada sounded pissed.

"Good morning to you, too." Gideon sounded exasperated.

"I've been calling and texting for two fucking hours. What is your goddamn problem that you can't shoot back one sentence that says you'll get back to me?"

"I'm getting back to you now. Your information this morning was good, by the way."

"It was fucking amazing. Now, let's start planning our next steps. Obviously, the two bozo cousins are in on it, so you need to squeeze them, but you saw how Bradley's older sister has to be in on it too, right? Her husband disappeared three years ago, and dollars to donuts his body is in a fifty-gallon barrel at the bottom of the swamp, and the sheriff is too scared to open any kind of case against her. I went through her bank records; she gets checks from the Holy Rosary Catholic Church in downtown Krotz

Springs for bookkeeping services, so she should have her ass in a pew today. Go get her."

Sebastian laughed and Gideon glared at him.

"Jada, you're not going to tell us how to handle things," Gideon all but growled.

"I damn well will if it will get Gianna back in one piece, or are you telling me that Sebastian's worthless uncle actually provided you with some information?"

"No," Gideon admitted.

"Where is he?" Jada demanded to know.

"He's currently spending some quality time tied up in a luxury apartment," Sebastian said with a satisfied smile. "We might check up on him if we have time, not that I really give a shit if we do."

Jada laughed. "Now that does my heart good."

"Are you finding the locations of properties like we asked?" Sebastian asked.

"I'll have all of that pretty soon. Are you going to get answers out of Bradley's sister and cousins?"

"Yep," Sebastian said succinctly.

"How? There's just the two of you."

"Jesus, Jada. We said we would take care of it! You need to mellow the fuck out."

Sebastian had rarely heard his friend so out of sorts.

"You need—"

"Shut it, Jada." Sebastian interrupted her. "We have a plan. There are more people than just Gideon and I working on this. Your intel on the sister is invaluable, and we'll let you know how it pans out. Text if you get anything new, but in the meantime, don't fucking blow up Gideon's phone just to get updates."

Gideon hung up. "You know she's going to call and text, right?"

"Can you blame her?" Sebastian asked. "But it seems

like she's doing good work. I think that we need to send Fergus over to the church."

"Why?"

"Out of the two brothers, he can charm his way in and out of any situation. Plus he's Catholic so he can handle the church environment."

"Okay," Gideon agreed. "And the cousins?"

"Did Jada get us the airboats and canoes like I asked?"

Gideon nodded. "Everything's been reserved, we just show up and take them."

"Okay, here's the plan. I need Neil and the team to pick up the boats and get them away from the rental place. I want them somewhere where we'll be able to stow one of Brad's relatives for questioning."

"Why are we going to question them on a boat?" Gideon asked.

"You'll see."

21

It sounded like the flapping of wings, a whine, a fan going at high speed. For the life of her, Gianna couldn't identify the sound but it was getting closer and closer.

It wasn't a motorboat—she'd been on the lake with her Pawpa and knew the sound—so what was it?

The noise wound down and she heard the distinct sound of footsteps splashing, then squishing through mud. The door flew open. It was Darrel. He grinned at her. Three cans from a six-pack of beer dangled from his finger in their plastic holder while he drank a fourth can. "You're awake."

She didn't say anything.

"You didn't die."

She just stared at him.

"Did you miss me?"

She continued to stare at him.

He threw his can of beer at her, forcing her to duck. "Bitch, say something!"

"What do you want me to say?"

He stalked over to her and grabbed her hair, hauling

her up so that she was on her knees. "I want you to tell me you're glad to see me."

Gianna forced back her sob of pain and whispered, "I'm glad to see you."

He thrust her away from him so that she bounced against the back of the couch. "Now that wasn't too hard, was it?" He pulled another can of beer from the six-pack rings and popped the top, not seeming to care when foam overflowed.

"Can't play with you yet. Brad's made that kind of clear. But he'll be done with you pretty soon." He took a sip of beer and crouched down in front of her. "Does that scare you, or make you hot?"

"Am I supposed to say something?"

Once again the high-pitched whine of a fan sounded in the distance. "Shit. We're going to have to wait to finish our little chat." Darnell shoved the can of beer at Gianna's face. "Want some?"

She turned her face away from him.

"You sure are uppity." He pulled back the beer and took a sip. "That's okay, you won't be by the time I'm done with you."

Gianna heard footsteps and hoped it was Bradley.

"Darnell, I don't have to kill you, do I?" Fontenot shouted as he barged into the cabin followed by the other man. Gianna couldn't remember his name.

Darnell stood up straight and turned around. "I'm the smart one, remember? I know how to take orders. What's more, I want my money more than I want a piece of tail."

"Quit calling me stupid," the skinny man whined.

"Jesus, Linus, quit sniveling, it makes you sound weak," Bradley sneered. "I say we film her from the couch today, what do you think Darnell?"

Darnell leered at Gianna, then looked at Fontenot. "Sounds good, cousin."

Bradley came closer to Gianna. "Today's Sunday. I know that your boy can't get his hands on the money til probably Tuesday or Wednesday at the soonest. Still, we want to give him some incentive. I need you looking a little more desperate than you did yesterday."

She wasn't going to give him the satisfaction of any kind of response.

"Hmmm, nothing to say, huh?"

"What do you have in mind?" Darnell asked.

"I need you to do the filming this time. Think you can handle that?" Fontenot asked Darnell as he handed him his phone.

"Sure thing."

"Make sure you don't get my face in the picture. Only hers. You got that?"

Darnell nodded.

Fontenot looked down at Gianna. "You're going to say, give Armand the money, otherwise they'll kill me. That's all you have to say. Got that? Nod if you understand me."

Gianna nodded.

Fontenot turned back to Darnell. "When I tell you to start filming, you start. When I tell you to stop filming, you stop."

Darnell nodded again.

"Okay, start."

Fontenot pointed at Gianna.

"Please give Armand the money, otherwise they'll kill me."

She saw Fontenot's hand fly back, but she didn't move in time. It crashed across her face.

"Ahhhhhhhh," she screamed as she fell off the couch.

The last thing she heard was, "Stop filming."

Meeting anyplace in Krotz Springs was risky; the town was just too damn small and too full of Fontenots. So Gideon suggested they go one town over to the Shooting Range. Neil and his boys, as well as the O'Malley brothers, had been busy.

"Bradley's dad is definitely mixed up in this," Neil said. The redheaded man next to him, named Red, nodded in agreement. "Leroy—that's his name—said he's going to buy out the Cajun Gator Tour Company next month. He's busy saying his boy is going to front him the money."

"The one cousin of his, Darnell isn't saying anything," Red said. "But he has that other convict, Linus, saying he and his cousin Bradley are doing big business together. He's always been the really stupid one in the family, according to everyone."

"Sounds like Bradley's dad is pretty damn dumb, if you ask me," Fergus O'Malley said with a laugh.

Sebastian looked down the firing line and made sure that nobody from the office was looking at their small huddle. They weren't.

"So, are we any closer to finding out where they may be keeping Gianna?" Gideon asked.

"I had a long talk with Selma after church this morning," Fergus said. "She does the books for most of the Fontenot family."

"She told you that?" Sebastian asked.

"Sure did. I told her how Callum and I were looking for an experienced bookkeeper, but we wanted one who understood the meaning of family. I made it sound like I was looking for somebody who was willing to cook the books, and she was all over that. The problem with her is that she won't have any real records of anything that isn't leased or owned. So all of the property that they're trespassing on won't be recorded, so we're shit out of luck."

"So we're back to scaring the shit out of Bradley, Linus, Darnell, or Bradley's father to find out where they've stashed Gianna," Callum said grimly.

"I'm down with that." Fergus slammed his fist into his other hand.

I really like these men.

"Let's go back to town and round up these assholes," Sebastian said as he looked over each man who surrounded him. Every one of the men nodded in agreement.

Gideon and Sebastian had already gone to Darnell and Linus' parents' house, as well as both of their trailers. When they'd knocked on Linus' trailer door, one of his neighbors had suggested that they try looking for him at Rory's Tavern. On the way there, they'd gotten calls from the O'Malley brothers who told them that they hadn't found any sign of Bradley anywhere in town. Meanwhile, Neil, Red, and the boys had been looking for Brad's father and had come up empty so far, but they were checking out a lead that he might be at the local auto body shop.

By the time Sebastian and Gideon had gotten to Rory's, they were told that Linus had just taken off to go fishing.

"Maybe Fergus can work his magic with Selma and find out where Linus fishes."

"It's worth a try," Gideon agreed as they started for the truck. When Sebastian settled into the passenger seat, he realized he'd missed a text. He sucked in a deep breath as he thumbed over the message to see who it was from. It was unknown, but it had a video attachment.

"What?" Gideon asked as he got into the driver's seat.

"Don't start the engine," Sebastian told him. "We have another video."

Gideon didn't say anything, he just leaned over to look as Sebastian pressed play.

Gianna's face came into view. Once again, she looked like she was pleading.

"Please give Armand the money, otherwise they'll kill me."

Sebastian watched in stunned disbelief as someone backhanded her. Gianna cried out and fell so that she was off-camera, then the video stopped. He closed his eyes, trying to stop the image from replaying itself in his mind.

"Bradley's trying to crawl into your head. You can't let him." Gideon clasped Sebastian's shoulder, but he shook off his friend's hand.

"Sebastian, you can't let him win."

"He's going to kill her, you know. This ransom is bullshit. He's planning to kill Armand, and yeah we can stop that. We can put the two of them behind bars. But if we don't find her, she's dead." Sebastian's voice was flat.

"Shake it off," Gideon bit out. "Call Fergus and see if he can find out Linus' fishing spot from Selma."

Sebastian nodded.

It was another two hours of nothing and then two things popped at once. Jada called and said she had a lock on Bradley Fontenot's mobile phone and Neil Hebert called and said that he, Red, and two of his boys had caught up with Leroy Fontenot and he was currently rolled up in a tarp in the back of Neil's pick-up. Neil told Sebastian where to meet them.

Sebastian looked over at Gideon. "Drop me off with Neil. I'm going to go confiscate Leroy's vehicle and use it as my own and see what I can do to find the cousins. In the meantime, you use Jada's info to track his ass."

Gideon nodded. As they started over across town, Sebastian's phone rang and the call went to the truck's Bluetooth. It was his grandfather

"When are you coming home, boy?"

"When I'm damn good and ready," Sebastian answered.

"That's not good enough. I delivered Armand, didn't I?"

"Your lousy son has more targets on him than a ten-point buck. You best be thinking about how to keep his sorry ass alive, not how to get me home and win an election."

"You're just listening to rumors. They've been going on for years, they mean nothing," his grandfather scoffed.

"This time they mean something. Look, Grandpère, I don't have time for this shit. I'm hanging up now."

"Wait!" the old man cried.

"What?"

"Bastian, I need you. They're telling me that without having you in the race, they won't back me for the lieutenant governor spot," he whispered. "I need their support."

"I'll talk to you when I get back home. We'll work something out."

Sebastian hung up.

"Why'd you keep him hanging like that?" Gideon asked. "I thought you were going to cut him off at the knees."

"I think I'll have a better shot of getting a confession from him about Gianna's mother if I keep him dangling on a thread."

"Makes sense."

"Why hasn't Jada just given us an address to go pick up Bradley?"

"His phone has to be off right now. As soon as he powers it back up, we'll have him. Jada's been monitoring this since she got his cell phone info downloaded."

Sebastian glanced over at Gideon. "Just how good is she?"

At the next stoplight, Gideon turned to face Sebastian fully. "There's a hell of a lot more to her than just her degrees. But according to her background, she had nothing to do with computers before attending NYU, and I don't buy it."

"She's been out of school for three years now. Couldn't she have picked all of this up during the four years at school and the three years since?" Sebastian asked.

"She's a natural, Sebastian. This is in her blood. She was plugged in long before college. I just need to figure out how."

Sebastian laughed. "Have you asked her?"

"No."

"Are you going to?"

"No."

"And you talk about my problems with communication."

22

Even though Sebastian had asked to rent only two-manned airboats, Neil and his boys had gotten ahold of a four-manned airboat, which would work out much better. Sebastian and Red were on the two-manned boat following Neil, Gunther, and Berle. In Neil's boat was the tarp that held Leroy Fontenot.

Sebastian hadn't piloted an airboat since he was seventeen, but it had all come back to him in minutes. Neil had set out at a slow and steady clip, so as not to draw suspicion, which Sebastian appreciated, but now that they'd been out on the swamp for a half-hour, Neil was steering them through thickets of trees, where not much could be seen. As Sebastian looked closer, he grinned. He saw the alligators up on the shore. Yep, Neil knew his shit.

They turned off their engines, and Sebastian threw over his rope to Berle so their boats could butt up against one another. Red took the first bucket of fresh meat and scattered it into the water. The alligators started to slither off the banks into the murky depths of the swamp.

"This is your show, boy." Neil nodded to Sebastian.

Berle and Sebastian switched boats, then Neil started unwrapping Leroy.

"Were you trying to kill me?" he screamed as soon as Sebastian pulled the duct tape off his mouth. "I could hardly breathe!"

"Not hardly. That isn't how I want you to die," Sebastian said flatly. "I have other plans for you."

"Shit. I know who you are. You don't scare me. You're going into politics like your granddaddy, you're not going to get your hands dirty." Leroy struggled to sit up now that he was no longer tied up in the tarp.

"Well, I guess you've heard part of my story. You know I grew up in the bayou, right?" Sebastian asked softly.

"Are you trying to scare me into thinking you're some kind of real Cajun? That you have balls?"

Sebastian smiled. "And I've been serving my country as a Navy SEAL, going in and out of countries you've never heard of, carrying out missions that nobody else could."

Leroy spit over the side of the boat. "So?"

"I have some questions for you."

Leroy grabbed his crotch. "Here's your answers. Suck my dick."

Sebastian pulled a large knife out of his boot, then looked over Leroy's shoulder and smiled. "Do you know what it means to chum the water?"

"Huh?"

"Look behind you, Leroy, we've got company."

Leroy jerked backward, trying to crabwalk when he saw two sets of eyes above the water.

Red laughed. "Those gators look big."

Sebastian didn't waste any time. He bent over and ran his knife down Leroy's thigh to his knee. No blood spurted, but it started to ooze.

"What the fuck?"

"You're going to be nothing more than chum to those gators. Here's how the questions will start. I ask you one. If you don't answer, I put your leg in the water and give the gators a chance to get ahold of it. If we can, we'll try to pull you back onto the boat so I can ask you the question one more time. If you fail to answer the second time, I'll cut your belly, then throw you overboard." Sebastian looked up at Neil. "Does that sound fair to you?"

"Yep." Neil's eyes glinted with anger. Yeah, he had a real fondness for Gianna too.

"You're Bastian right?" Leroy asked, his eyes wide as he tried to stem the flow of blood on his leg. "Bastian Durand. I'll tell you anything you want. Anything. Just ask me," he begged.

"Do you believe he'll tell me the truth?" Sebastian asked Neil.

"No, I don't."

"I will." Leroy pushed up and grabbed at Sebastian's pant leg. "I will. Whatever you want to know," he choked out. "Whatever you want to know, I'll tell you." His words ended with a sob.

"Okay, where is your son hiding the girl?"

Leroy coughed. He wiped his eyes then looked back up at Sebastian. "It's hard to explain where."

He either didn't know, or he'd decided not to cooperate. He nodded to Neil and Red. Sebastian grabbed Leroy around his upper chest, Red grabbed one arm, and Neil grabbed the other. They lifted him up and Leroy started to kick.

"Nooooooo!" he wailed. "I can explain how to get to the cabin. I swear."

Sebastian and the two other men worked as a team and lowered Leroy toward the water. He pulled his knees up to his chest. "I'll take you to her. I swear it. Let me take you to her." Sebastian wrinkled his nose as he smelled urine.

He gave a chin lift to Neil and Red, and the three of them lifted Leroy back into the middle of the boat.

"Take us there."

It was the third shack that Leroy had directed them to. Each time they'd come even close to one of the cabins, Neil would duct tape and roll Leroy back into the tarp, then they'd shut off the engines and start poling so they wouldn't make any noise. These men were damn near as quiet as his teammates, and like his teammates, they were all armed. Sebastian prayed that this cabin would be the one where he would finally find Gianna.

There were windows on the east and west side of the shack. They were covered by thick, clear plastic, but that would do. Sebastian was on point. He made his way up to the first window and peeked in. It was dim inside, but he was still able to see the entire space, and except for a few pieces of furniture, it was empty.

Dammit.

"It's empty," he yelled out.

This entire operation was a bust. He turned to Neil. "We've got three legitimate properties that the Fontenot family own. The O'Malley brothers have been checking those out. We'll go back to town and see if they've found anything."

"What do we do with Bradley's father?" Neil asked.

"Leave him here," Sebastian said. "Just duct tape his wrists. It should only take him three or four days to get back home, and by that time we'll be done."

"Got it."

It was damn near midnight when he got back to Krotz Springs and had cell service again. He had three texts from Gideon telling him to call and two voicemails from his grandfather. He'd sent everyone else back to Baton Rouge to get some shut-eye at the motel.

"What's up?" he asked his friend when he answered as he yawned. He pulled Leroy's keys out of his pocket and looked at the brown Cutlass Oldsmobile and shook his head. He went over to it and tried the handle. It was locked. It took him a moment to figure out which key was needed to unlock the car.

"Bradley Fontenot's phone is back in Baton Rouge, specifically at the Blonde Bayou."

"When did you find that out?" Sebastian asked as he got into the car and pushed back the seat.

"Fifteen minutes ago."

"Do you need me to go with you?" Sebastian asked as he put the phone on speaker and set it on the car's bench seat.

"Why don't you want to go?"

"She was hurting two days ago. You could see Gianna had already been hit in the face. Then yesterday's hit? No. Absolutely not. I can't leave, Gideon. I've got to find her now. I'm really worried."

"What's your plan?"

"The legit properties were a bust, right?"

"Yep," Gideon answered.

"Then I'm going to go let myself into the two cousin's trailers, have a look around. Then if they're not there, I'm going to wait for them."

"I think that could work," Gideon agreed.

"Keep me informed on what's going on." Sebastian put the old land cruiser into drive and headed down the street.

"I will." Gideon hung up and Sebastian shoved his phone back into his pocket before it fell onto the car floor. The trailer park where both men lived was three miles outside of town. Sebastian felt comfortable driving the car into the park and parking in one of the free slots. This car fit right in. He took a long look around, then got out and meandered toward Darnell's trailer. Three homes down, young men and women were sitting outside on cheap white chairs smoking joints, the marijuana smell drifting all the way to him. None of them were paying Sebastian any attention.

He got out his lock-pick set, but first tried the door. It was open. He let himself in. The place was as neat as a pin. It took Sebastian mere moments to check every nook and cranny to ensure that Darnell was not inside. Then he did a much more thorough check, looking for anything that might provide a clue to indicate where Gianna was being held. He did pocket Darnell's Smith and Wesson 9mm. He was sure he had another pistol on him at the moment, but there was no reason to let him have any more firepower.

It was time to check out Linus' place. When he let himself out, he didn't even bother to look over at the young crowd. Instead, he just went three rows over and down a few houses, until he hit the trailer that belonged to Linus. Just by the shape of the outside—with the dilapidated porch, the fence that was hanging off its hinges, and the dead grass—Sebastian knew Linus' trailer would not be neat as a pin.

He tried the door but it was locked. It took him less than a minute to let himself inside. Once again he first made a check and found no sign of Linus, then he did a more thorough search. Under his bed, Sebastian found two AR-15s, one AK-47, a Glock, and a whole hell of a lot of ammo. Taking all of that out to the car was going to be kind of obvious, so Sebastian took all of the ammunition out of the rifles and the pistol, as well as the additional ammo and cartridges, and brought them into the living room. He looked around for a moment, then he remembered.

Sebastian went back outside and looked at the obviously broken grill and opened the lid. He threw all the cartridges inside and shut the lid. That done, he wandered back to the Cutlass. He drove it right outside the entrance of the trailer park, maneuvering it so that the two driver's side wheels sat in the gulley on the side of the road. Hopefully, anybody looking at the car would think it was stuck and that's why it was sitting there.

As for Sebastian, he was just a poor bastard who was sleeping in his stuck car until morning, probably drunk. Yep, that would work.

He called Jada and it went to voicemail but he didn't leave a message.

He texted her, telling her to call him. She didn't.

He called her again.

"Can't a girl go to the bathroom? Seriously, first, you tell me not to bother you guys, then you act like your ass is on fire. Mellow. It was less than two minutes. A girl needs to pee occasionally."

"I need to know what the two Fontenot brothers drive."

"A 'hello' and a 'please' would go a long way."

"We don't have time to fuck around."

"Goddammit, Sebastian, I'm *not* fucking around. I'm already starting the search, all right? I'm trying to do things. Actual productive work that will help my friend, instead of pulling all the stuffing out of my pillow or crying!"

"Jada—"

"Darnell doesn't have a car. He rides a motorcycle, a

Yamaha Volt. I'm sending you a picture right now. And surprise, surprise, surprise, a man from Louisiana owns a truck. Who woulda thunk it? Linus' ride is a red RAM-1500."

"Sounds a lot like all of his rifle choices," Sebastian mumbled.

"What?"

"Never mind."

"Thanks, Jada."

"Sebastian?" Ah, shit, he could actually hear a tremor in her voice.

"Yeah?"

"Please tell me you're close to finding her."

"We are."

"She looks really bad, and after that last hit…"

Sebastian sat up in his seat. "How do you know about her being hit?" he demanded to know. "Did you hack into my phone? How in the fuck did you hack into my phone?"

"Who cares? I saw the videos, that's what matters. Please find her."

He raked his fingers through his hair, yanking at the back ends. "I will. I promise."

"That's good."

He hung up the phone and slumped back down in his seat. After an hour and a half passed only two vehicles had come in to the park. He texted Gideon but got no response. His gut was churning; he hadn't eaten since Neil had shoved food at him before they'd gotten in the airboats. Shit, he knew better than that.

He heard the rumble of a motorcycle and his heart started beating fast. The driver took the turn fast into the trailer park, but even from here, Sebastian could see the bike matched the picture that Jada had sent. Darnell had arrived.

Sebastian eased the car out of the ditch and slowly drove back into the park and toward Darnell's trailer. The little party three doors down had dispersed, so that was good news. When he saw the man go inside, he parked beside his house. He needed to be close since Darnell would be coming on a little drive with him.

Sebastian knew the layout of his home, so he took a shot that he'd be headed for either the kitchen or a shower and bed. So he went around back and peeked up into the kitchen window. No sign of Darnell. When he went around to the side, he didn't see him in the back bedroom either, but the door to the bathroom was now closed, and it had been partially open before. Sebastian hustled to the front door.

"Son of a bitch," he hissed when he found the door locked. He pulled out his lock-pick set and let himself in. He went over to a kitchen drawer and pulled out the roll of duct tape he'd seen. He pulled off a strip, then took out his Glock 19 and went to the bathroom door. He hoped like hell that Darnell would come out dressed; it would make all of this so much easier. The door opened, and Sebastian cursed.

"Hands up."

"What the hell?" Darnell screeched as he dropped his towel.

"I won't say it again, hands on the back of your head. You know the damned drill."

"You can't come into my home—" Darnell started.

Sebastian grabbed him by his wet hair and slapped the duct tape over his mouth.

"You're going to get dressed. Then you and I are going to go for a little ride. Got it?"

Darnell took a swing at him. In the cramped hallway, there wasn't much power behind it. Sebastian pulled

Darnell's swinging arm towards him and shoved the hand into the wall. Sebastian heard the sound of bones breaking. Darnell lowered his head, aiming at Sebastian's chest. Sebastian side-stepped, this time shoving Darnell so hard into the wall that his head broke through to the bathroom. Sebastian wrenched him out of the wall and Darnell slumped to his knees with the pain.

"Let's try this again. You're going to get dressed, then we're going to go on a little ride. Nod if you've got me."

Darnell looked up at him, his eyes dazed.

"I said nod."

Darnell nodded.

Sebastian followed him into his bedroom and watched as he attempted to get dressed with broken fingers. It took a long time. When he was done, Sebastian grabbed his wounded hand and twisted, then shoved it up Darnell's back, marching him to the living room.

"Darnell, you're going to tell me where Gianna is. You don't, I'm going to shoot your kneecap. I'm going to ask you a second time. You don't tell me again, I'll shoot your second knee. That will have been your last chance, because the third shot will be your crotch and you'll bleed out. It won't be pleasant. Are you hearing me?"

Darnell nodded.

"Good," Sebastian smiled.

They went out to the car and Sebastian shoved Darnell into the passenger seat, where he huddled against the door. They got to where they'd left the airboats in record time.

Sebastian's phone pinged. He was so close to success, he wanted to ignore it, but that would be stupid. He looked at the text. It was from Gideon.

Call me.

23

"Yeah?" Sebastian asked. "Did you find him?"

"No sign of him, and per Jada he's powered down his phone again so he could be anywhere."

"It's oh-three-hundred. He should be in bed," Sebastian said.

"Where are you?" Gideon asked.

"I've got Darnell with me. He's going to show me where Gianna is."

"For real?"

"Yep."

"What about the other cousin, do you have a bead on him?"

"No," Sebastian admitted.

"So he or Bradley could be waiting for you."

"I know. But I gotta do this."

"Wait for me," Gideon said, his voice full of command. Figured, since he was second in command of the Omega Sky team.

"I can't, Gideon. I don't know how badly she's been hurt. I've got to go now. Jada's hacked my phone; have her do her voodoo and track me once you get here. Grab Neil and the boys—they'll show you how to pilot an airboat."

"Don't go!"

"Sorry, I think this connection is bad." Sebastian hung up the phone. He reached over Darnell and opened the door, then shoved the bastard out onto the ground, scooted across the bench seat, and got out behind him.

He picked him up off the ground and practically dragged him down the path to the edge of the swamp. Sebastian pointed to the four-man airboat. "Hop on."

Before he started the airboat's engine, Sebastian took the roll of duct tape and used it to bind Darnell's wrists behind his back. Then he ripped the tape off his mouth. He was crying.

Sebastian settled his gun against Darnell's kneecap. "Do you remember our little talk back at your trailer?"

"Yes, sir."

"I want you to direct me to where Gianna is. Personally, I'd trust you more if you were bleeding all over the bottom of the boat. What do you think? Should I shoot you first before you start giving me directions?"

Sebastian resisted the urge to roll his eyes when all Darnell did was stare.

"That was a question."

"Yes, sir."

"Oh, fuck it. Tell me which direction to go."

Darnell lifted his head from the bottom of the boat, obviously confused. "I don't know. I can only do this when I'm in the chair."

Sebastian hoisted Darnell into the airboat chair then duct-taped him to it. He was pretty sure the dumbass wouldn't try to get away by jumping into the swamp when his hands were taped behind his back, but who the hell knew.

"Which way?"

Darnell tilted his head straight. "Straight ahead, then veer left after that big cypress."

It took forty minutes of twists and turns before Sebastian saw an airboat up ahead.

"Who's there?" Sebastian demanded to know.

"I don't know."

"You say one wrong thing, and I won't start with your kneecaps, I'm aiming for your dick, you got it?"

Sebastian pulled in as close as he could to shore and anchored the boat.

A voice came from the shack. "Bradley? Darnell? I got here as fast as I could. I did good, right?"

Well, that answered that question. It was Linus.

Sebastian watched a man walk out of the cabin. He couldn't see if he was holding a weapon, so he just let him come closer. "I don't think she's all right."

Sebastian's gut clenched.

Linus kept coming closer. His hands were at his sides, empty. "I gave her some water and food like you said, Brad, but she threw it up."

He came closer. Sebastian aimed and shot a bullet right in front of his feet.

Linus jumped. "What? Are you trying to kill me?"

"Get down on your knees, put your hands behind your neck. Do it now."

Linus crashed to his knees. "Please don't shoot me."

Sebastian got out of the boat with the duct tape. When he got to the man, he kicked his face down into the mud, then taped his wrists together. The absolute second he was done he ran up to the cabin and shoved open the door.

His heart stopped.

Matted hair. A tied-up, contorted body that was so still. He dropped his gun and grabbed his knife out of his boot.

"Gianna. *Cher.* Wake up," he crooned.

He sawed the ropes off her wrists and ankles, desperately trying not to cause any more injury, all the while whispering to her, begging her to wake up, telling her how much she meant to him. Pleading with her to open her beautiful eyes.

Sebastian picked up his gun, then gently picked her up and carried her out of the cabin. He so wanted to kill the two men who had hurt her, but he didn't. He splashed through the marsh and placed her gently on the bottom of the four-man airboat where Darnell was still sitting. He would have loved nothing better than to leave him behind like Linus, but he needed his help guiding them out of the swamp. He needed to get Gianna to a hospital as quickly as possible. He kept her cradled in his arms as he piloted the boat back to the landing, all the while checking his cell phone for coverage. When he finally had a signal, he called 9-1-1.

When Sebastian got to the landing, Neil, the O'Malley brothers, and the rest of the boys were there, as was an ambulance. It wasn't until he saw Gianna rushed past the emergency room bay doors that he was able to turn to Neil and ask him how he knew to be there. Neil explained that a woman named Jada had called him.

"Neil, call her back. Tell her what's happening."

Sebastian grabbed the arm of a nurse. "What's going on back there with Gianna?"

"Who?"

"Gianna Prentiss? She came in the ambulance five minutes ago with a head injury. She's alive but unresponsive. They took her back there. What's going on?"

"Are you family?"

"I'm her fiancée," he immediately lied.

She looked over her shoulder, then looked back at him. "I'll see what I can find out."

Sebastian paced the length of the emergency room lobby, blocking out all of the other people. He didn't know how long he had been walking back and forth until Fergus O'Malley grabbed his arm and forced him into a chair. "You're not doing anybody any good this way."

"Somebody needs to get their ass out here and tell me what is going on."

"Sebastian!" a voice called. He shot up out of the chair and looked at the emergency bay doors. He couldn't tell what was going on with Gideon; he couldn't read him at all.

"How is she?" Gideon asked as he marched over to him.

"I don't fucking know. Nobody will tell me anything." Sebastian raked his fingers through his hair and pulled.

"Okay, don't worry. I'll find out." Gideon patted his shoulder and walked away.

Sebastian watched as he walked up to the same desk he'd been disrupting for the last half hour. Gideon came back to him with a clipboard. He was frowning.

"We need to go upstairs. She's been admitted. They're doing surgery."

Sebastian couldn't breathe. What was he talking about?

"Surgery for what?" Fergus asked. "Did they say?"

"A brain bleed. We need to get upstairs to the waiting room. They said the surgeon would come and inform her fiancée. They also need her insurance information."

"Fuck that noise," Fergus growled.

"What floor?" Sebastian asked.

"Seven."

She loved the sun. She adored the sun. How come it hurt so much?

Gianna tried to open her eyes again, but again she whimpered. When had the sun become her enemy?

"Gianna, can you hear me?"

She felt pressure on her hand. It was warm and nice. She grabbed on tight. It was Sebastian. He was threading their fingers together, palm to palm. She tried to lift her lids, but the light was just too much.

"Hurts," she mumbled.

"What hurts, *cher*?" he asked.

"The sunshine."

He let go of her hand and even behind her eyelids she could feel the room darken. She still kept her eyes closed anyway. "I'm in the hospital, aren't I?"

"Yes, you are."

She turned her head toward his voice, then gasped in pain.

"Don't move your head. You were operated on a few days ago, and they just brought you out of a coma."

"A coma?"

"It was medically induced. They wanted the swelling in your brain to go down," Sebastian whispered.

Gianna heard herself breathing fast and hard as she took in the information. Sebastian took her hand again, this time stroking circles in the middle of her palm. "Are you calmer now?"

"I think so. Am I going to be all right?"

"The doctors say you'll make a complete recovery," he assured her.

She sighed.

"Now, will you open your beautiful eyes for me? I've been so scared."

Her lip tilted up. "You don't get scared."

"Yes, I do."

She opened her eyes. She saw his brimming with tears.

"Sebastian," she whispered. "Please, no. What's wrong?"

"I almost lost you, and I hardly had you."

"What are you talking about?" He wasn't making any sense.

Sebastian lowered his head and brushed his lips against hers. He lifted up and looked into her eyes. He must have seen her acceptance because he dipped down again and captured her face with both hands and kissed her like his life depended on it.

He jerked his head up. "I'm sorry, *cher*."

"For what?"

He gave a wry chuckle. "You just woke up from a coma. I shouldn't be kissing you like that."

"Like what?"

"Like I want to live all of my tomorrows with you."

Her eyes widened so much she thought they might pop out of her head. "Am I still in a coma?"

"Gianna, I've been the one who's lived my life in a coma. But now I know that life's too short. I love you with my whole heart."

"You do?"

"I want to live the rest of my life with you."

She shook her head and gasped in pain.

"*Cher*, stop that. Why are you shaking your head?"

"I'm trying to clear it. Trying to see if this is real or not."

"It is. I'm laying all of my feelings on the line, my entire heart. I want so much for you to say you love me too, but it's more important that you know how much I love you.

You need to know just how much I cherish you. I will always treasure you, Gianna. Know that."

She'd been needing to hear those words her whole life. She needed someone to give her the gift of their love and not expect anything in return, and somehow it was this amazing man.

"Thank you, Sebastian."

He softly rested his forehead against hers. "No, thank you. Thank you for teaching me how to love, cherish, and trust."

She tried to reach up and touch him, but her hands were connected to I.V.s. "Sebastian?" she whispered.

"Yes, *cher*?"

"I love you too. With all my heart."

EPILOGUE

FIVE WEEKS LATER

Sebastian hadn't expected to be back in Louisiana so soon. He knew he was going to need to be here for the trials, but here he was. He couldn't believe everything that had happened since Hurricane Helen had hit. He grinned as he looked down at the group text that Blessing had sent all of them. The woman he'd met at the airport so long ago was kind of spooky. But, she'd been right; he actually had found his home, just not the way he'd expected.

He scrolled through to the next text and saw the one sent directly to him from his fellow SEAL, Kyle Jones out of Coronado. The man had sent him a picture. Kyle was actually smiling, and the woman in his arms was beautiful. It looked like life had turned around for both of them.

He looked up when the door to the carriage house opened.

"Dammit, Gianna, don't tell me you drove straight through!" He strode across the little living room and hauled her up against him, his body trembling with worry. "You weren't supposed to be here for two more days."

She giggled up at him. "I didn't drive, Jada did. It's all good."

Sebastian leaned around her to look out the door. He didn't see anyone. "Where is she?"

"She's at Jimmy's Po-Boy's and getting some beignets. She's going to go spend some time with Ophelia and stay at the big house."

Sebastian frowned. He wasn't sure how he felt about Jada horning in on his time with Gianna, but he was getting some extra days with her, so there was that.

"So, did you get everything straightened out with the lawyer?" she asked.

Sebastian ran his fingers through his hair and blew out a breath. "I'm not sure how this is going to go, but yes I did. He said it was all pretty straightforward and wasn't a problem. I have the letter and the transfer deed over there on the counter. Are you sure they're going to be okay with it?"

Gianna giggled. "They're going to be fine with it. And if they're not, they can sell the damn place."

"I'm really sick of lawyers," Sebastian muttered as he stared down at Gianna's lips.

"And cops, don't forget them."

"How about the district attorney's office?" Sebastian said. "I'm sick of the A.D.A. and the D.A."

"I vote for being sick of the F.B.I." She grinned.

"But seriously, do you think Philly and Neil are going to be okay with this? Maybe I should have just given them money."

Gianna turned around and closed the door. She grabbed Sebastian's hand and practically dragged him to the sofa. "Sit down," she commanded as she shoved at his chest.

He sat down, and then she straddled his lap. "Now listen to me."

"I'm listening."

"Remember how upset you were when I told you about how much your Grinch of a grandfather was paying Neil and Ophelia?"

Sebastian nodded. "That's why when I came into all that coin it only seemed fair to cut them in on it."

Gianna rolled her eyes. "I said for you to listen. You're talking."

He smiled again, his eyes twinkling as he gripped her ass. "Okay, I'm listening now, I promise."

"How many years has Ophelia loved and honored this place?" Gianna asked softly. "Ophelia caretaking this home, and Neil caring for the land?"

"Over thirty," Sebastian whispered.

"And you remember Neil telling you that his dad used to work part of this before it all got bought up by the Durands, right?"

Sebastian nodded.

"This is what you want to do, isn't it?"

Sebastian nodded again.

"Then honey, you're doing the right thing. Giving them this property is what they'll want. Now it will be their decision what they do with it. They can sell it, they can give it to their grandkids, they can build a strip mall on it. But after everything they've done, this is theirs."

Sebastian brushed back the curls from Gianna's face. "Okay, you've convinced me. So let's talk about more important things. How are you doing with untangling yourself with Tina's Treasures?"

Gianna's face fell and Sebastian did his best not to react. "What's going on?"

"It's not the shop. I wanted to wait to discuss this with you when we were together. Granny took a fall last week.

She's up now, but having to use a walker. We're having to get her into physical therapy three times a week."

"We?" Sebastian asked.

"Okay, me."

Sebastian's fingers clenched into her soft flesh. "Is there anything I can do to help?" he asked.

Gianna gave him a wavering smile and bit her lip. "Be patient with me? You know I want to move to Virginia, but I can't leave my grandparents right now. Not when Granny needs me."

Sebastian nodded. "I get it."

She leaned down and kissed him. "I love you, honey."

"I love you too, *cher.*"

Six Months Later

Gianna looked around the dining room of Neil and Ophelia's house. It looked so much different than when it was the Durand house. It was actually welcoming. Well, it would have been, except for the tired faces of the people surrounding the table.

Gianna held out her hand, palm up and Sebastian grabbed it. He twined their fingers together.

"I'm sorry you had to testify, *cher,*" Sebastian said for the hundredth time.

"Honey, I wanted to testify," Gianna said for the hundred-and-first time.

"One trial down, one more to go," Jada grinned. Sebastian's hand tensed in hers.

"Shut up, Jada."

"Hey, it could have been worse. Bradley could've lived and he could have gone on trial too," Jada said. "Instead, it's just your uncle and granddad. And only if your granddad makes it out of the hospital since his health took a turn for the worse, so there really might only be one."

"Jesus, Jada, shut the fuck up!" Gianna shouted at her friend.

All eyes turned to her.

"Are you okay honey?" Ophelia asked tentatively.

Gianna hit her head against the dining room table. "I guess it kind of shows that I'm out of sorts if I swear, huh?"

"Actually, it does," Gideon said with a smile in his voice.

"I hate Armand Durand. I hate him. I hate him. I hate him." Gianna wrenched her hand from Sebastian's and shot up out of her chair. She backed up against the dining room wall and stared at everyone. "How could someone be so evil and greedy? How?"

All those months ago it had taken a little unraveling, but Gideon had found a bank account under Pamela Durand's name that had been opened as soon as she had divorced Sebastian the Third. Her ex-husband had put a lump sum of a million dollars into the account upon their divorce, and then twenty-five thousand a month. By the time of her death, over three million dollars would have been deposited into the account. None of it had ever been accessed by Pamela Durand, yet the account was empty.

Sebastian got up from the table and pulled Gianna into his arms. "*Cher*, please, this isn't good for the little one, huh?" He touched the small swell of her belly.

"But he had your mom and dad killed for money." Gianna gripped the front of Sebastian's shirt and smashed her face against it, hating that she was crying yet again. That's all she ever did these days.

"But he's going to be brought to justice," Sebastian said as he stroked her hair.

She turned her head so she could look at Jada and

Gideon. They were the ones who had helped figure everything out. The first Sebastian Durand had given both of his grandsons millions and millions of dollars in trust funds. Armand had gambled all of his away by the time his brother was getting a divorce, so he offered his brother help to set up an account for his ex-wife. Then when Armand spent all of that money, he needed more. He needed his brother's money, so he figured he'd work a deal with the family lawyer and make sure the little orphan's money came Armand's way.

Jada got up from her seat and pulled Gianna gently from Sebastian's arms. She was crying. "I'm so sorry we can't get justice for your mama," she whispered into Gianna's hair.

Gianna shook her head and smiled at her friend. "It's okay. We know Lazar did something to make her go away, and that had to be the reason she ended up strung out on drugs and with my father."

"We'll find out what happened, I promise, even if he dies before he pays," Jada's eyes glittered.

Gideon stood up from his chair. "After the house of cards toppled and people found out how he stole Sebastian's inheritance, people came out of the woodwork to point fingers at him."

"So, Gianna, don't worry, he'll go to prison," Ophelia spoke up.

Nobody said anything.

Ophelia looked around the room. "Lazar will end up in prison, won't he? Please say he will."

Gianna was back in Sebastian's arms, his hand resting on her stomach. "I'm sorry, Philly, it's not likely. His lawyers are going to make this drag out forever, and with his current health conditions, ten to one says he dies a free man."

Gianna let out a sob.

"But that's not fair. He's the one who killed Gianna's mom," Ophelia wailed.

"There were others involved in all of this," Gideon said. "And we're going to find them."

Five Months Later

Sebastian cuddled his wife closer to him on the hospital bed. It was a tight fit, but it worked. When the nurse came in, she gave an exasperated grin.

"Have you decided on a name for this little guy?"

Sebastian tucked back one of Gianna's wayward curls and grinned when she giggled.

"Don't say it," Sebastian warned.

"How about—"

The nurse came forward and handed Gianna their son. Sebastian felt his heart flip over in his chest. Neither of them noticed as she left the room.

"He looks like you," Gianna sighed right before she yawned. "I really think his name should be—"

Sebastian covered her mouth with his hand. Her eyes twinkled up at him. She bit his fingers. When he lifted his hand and shook it, she burst out with, "Sebastian Lazar Durand the Fifth."

"All right, you said it. You are so going to be punished in six weeks," he growled.

She laughed out loud again.

"Now, which name is it really?"

"Neil Gideon Durand," Gianna said.

Sebastian smoothed the hair on his son's head. "That's a perfect name."

For the next Long Road Home adventures, click below!

Home Front by Cat Johnson
My Heart's Home by Kris Michaels
Home to Stay by Maryann Jordan
Finding Home by Abbie Zanders

If you want to read Gideon and Jada's story, click here:
If you're interested to hear about Kostya, click here:

ABOUT THE AUTHOR

Caitlyn O'Leary is a USA Bestselling Author, #1 Amazon Bestselling Author and a Golden Quill Recipient from Book Viral in 2015. Hampered with a mild form of dyslexia she began memorizing books at an early age until her grandmother, the English teacher, took the time to teach her to read -- then she never stopped. She began re-writing alternate endings for her Trixie Belden books into happily-ever-afters with Trixie's platonic friend Jim. When she was home with pneumonia at twelve, she read the entire set of World Book Encyclopedias -- a little more challenging to end those happily.

Caitlyn loves writing about Alpha males with strong heroines who keep the men on their toes. There is plenty of action, suspense and humor in her books. She is never shy about tackling some of today's tough and relevant issues.

In addition to being an award-winning author of romantic suspense novels, she is a devoted aunt, an avid reader, a former corporate executive for a Fortune 100 company, and totally in love with her husband of soon-to-be twenty years.

She recently moved back home to the Pacific North-west from Southern California. She is so happy to see the seasons again; rain, rain and more rain. She has a large fan group on Facebook and through her e-mail list. Caitlyn is known for telling her "Caitlyn Factors", where she relates her little and big life's screw-ups. The list is long. She loves hearing and connecting with her fans on a daily basis.

Keep up with Caitlyn O'Leary:

Website: www.caitlynoleary.com
FB Reader Group: http://bit.ly/2NUZVjF
Email: caitlyn@caitlynoleary.com
Newsletter: http://bit.ly/1WIhRup

facebook.com/Caitlyn-OLeary-Author-638771522866740
twitter.com/CaitlynOLearyNA
instagram.com/caitlynoleary_author
amazon.com/author/caitlynoleary
bookbub.com/authors/caitlyn-o-leary
goodreads.com/CaitlynOLeary
pinterest.com/caitlynoleary35

ALSO BY CAITLYN O'LEARY

Night Storm Series

Her Ruthless Protector (Book #1)

Her Tempting Protector (Book #2)

Her Chosen Protector (Book #3)

Her Intense Protector (Book #4)

Her Sensual Protector (Book #5)

Her Faithful Protector (Book #6)

Her Noble Protector (Book #7)

Her Righteous Protector (Book #8)

Night Storm Legacy Series

Lawson & Jill (Book 1)

The Midnight Delta Series

Her Vigilant Seal (Book #1)

Her Loyal Seal (Book #2)

Her Adoring Seal (Book #3)

Sealed with a Kiss (Book #4)

Her Daring Seal (Book #5)

Her Fierce Seal (Book #6)

A Seals Vigilant Heart (Book #7)

Her Dominant Seal (Book #8)

Her Relentless Seal (Book #9)

Her Treasured Seal (Book #10)

Her Unbroken Seal (Book #11)

Black Dawn Series

Her Steadfast Hero (Book #1)

Her Devoted Hero (Book #2)

Her Passionate Hero (Book #3)

Her Wicked Hero (Book #4)

Her Guarded Hero (Book #5)

Her Captivated Hero (Book #6)

Her Honorable Hero (Book #7)

Her Loving Hero (Book #8)

The Found Series

Revealed (Book #1)

Forsaken (Book #2)

Healed (Book #3)

Shadows Alliance Series

Declan

Made in the USA
Las Vegas, NV
10 November 2023